THE DRAGON

VALENTINE

BOOK 3

KIMBERLY LOTH

Cover design by Rebecca Frank

Interior design by Colleen Sheehan
Write Dream Repeat Book Design LLC

For Matt
For being my second father

CHAPTER 1

IT DIDN'T MATTER how often she made this journey, Hazel didn't like the flight home or, for that matter, waiting in crowded airports. Especially when she was flying standby. She felt so out of control. Today was even worse since she was going home to search for her brother. That was something she never thought she'd do. She always figured she'd have to fly to the mainland because Aspen had gotten into trouble. But Rowan? He never left the house.

Guilt pricked at her insides. Even after living in Hawaii for two years, she wondered if she'd made the right choice. Her family was super close, and no one understood why she went so far away. Not that she would expect them to understand. Maybe if she'd stayed home, Rowan would've never gone missing. But then she'd probably be married and stuck in Montana forever.

Though if she'd never left, she would've been able to help. Her parents waited a whole week to let her know he was missing in the wilds of Yellowstone. In the middle of a freezing cold January. The chances that he was still alive were slim to none. She took a couple of deep breaths, inhaling the smell of pizza from the restaurant across the hall, and approached the gate counter again. A new gate agent had replaced the one she talked to fifteen minutes ago. He was young. Cute too. Dirty blonde hair and wide eyes.

"Excuse me," she said, and he looked up. Time to turn on the charm. She bit her lip and fiddled with the neckline of her shirt. "I really need to get on this flight." She dipped her head so she could catch his eye and let him know she'd caught him staring at her breasts. The trick didn't usually work. She'd been told her green eyes captivated most people, and they never bothered to look anywhere else, but she had more success with guys who took time to check out the rest of her slim figure. Match that with her jet black hair, and she earned the nickname Snow White in high school. But it didn't fit anymore because she was too tan.

He blushed and looked down at his computer screen. "What's your name?"

"Hazel Winters." She almost reached over and touched the back of his hand but decided that might be going a bit far.

"I'm sorry, ma'am, but you'll have to wait until we see if there are any seats left after the final boarding call. You're number one on standby, but right now the flight is completely full." He said all this without looking at her. Plus he called her ma'am. Dammit. She'd have try something else. She summoned a few tears and sniffed.

"You don't understand. My brother is missing, and I need to get home to help find him. This is the last flight out that will get me a connecting flight home. Please."

He looked up, and his face softened. She knew she'd gotten to him. He plucked a few tissues out from under the counter and handed them to her.

"I'll see what I can do."

"Thank you," she said, bringing the tissues up to her nose and lowering her eyelashes. She turned and found a chair as close as possible to the counter and stared at the cute gate agent. Unfortunately, it was under the air conditioner, and within seconds she was freezing. In her rush, she'd forgotten her hoodie.

Every time he looked over at her, she dropped her gaze and played with her hair. Slowly, the seats around her emptied, and the line at the gate disappeared. The agent at the counter got on the loud speaker.

"This is final boarding call for Flight 342 to San Francisco."

Hazel jumped up.

"Can I get a seat now?"

He looked at her apologetically. "There's still one seat left, but it belongs to someone. If they don't show up in the next three minutes, it's all yours."

Hazel sat down and kept a close eye on the clock. One minute ticked by, then two, then three. As soon as the clock ticked to eight twenty-two, Hazel was back at the counter.

The agent handed her a boarding pass and winked. "First class. Have a nice flight."

"Thank you," Hazel said with a grateful grin, and raced down the jetway.

First class. Miracles did exist. Or it was her flirting skills. He could've just as easily upgraded someone else and put her back in coach.

She didn't bother to look at her seat assignment until she stepped onto the plane. Three C. She'd never sat so far up, especially on a flight from Hawaii to the mainland.

She put her suitcase in the overhead compartment, collapsed into the aisle seat, buckled her seatbelt, closed her eyes, and let out a breath of relief. She made it. She rubbed her hands along the edge of her seat, feeling the soft leather. This was way nicer than the scratchy seats back in coach.

She'd been so nervous about making the flight she hadn't worried about the gazillion other things. Like how she'd have to repeat this entire semester and that her brother was out there somewhere in the frozen woods. Alone. In sub-zero temperatures.

"Hello," a soft voice said to her.

Oh great, she was next to a stranger who wanted to *talk*. She had to spend the next six hours sitting next to him, so she didn't want to be rude. She took another deep breath, opened her eyes, and smiled.

"Hi," she said, and her breath caught in her throat. She was sitting next to the most beautiful man she'd ever laid eyes on. That was saying a lot since she spent nearly every Saturday and Sunday out on the water with some gorgeous surfer boys.

Deep brown eyes and eyelashes that went on for miles. He had shaggy dark hair and bronze skin. A chiseled jaw and completely kissable lips. Hazel almost laughed. She shouldn't be thinking about kissing anyone right now. In any other circumstance, she'd be turning on the charm. She forced herself to look away from his face. He wore a short sleeved red polo shirt that revealed toned arms. He had on flip-flops and khaki shorts. Probably a rich boy visiting Hawaii on his way home to Cali. He'd be a nice distraction on the plane. Though, he had a book on his lap. He might not want to talk to her.

"Are you scared of flying?" he asked with a nod toward her hands gripping the armrests. She hadn't even noticed. These were just as rough as the ones back in coach though.

She tried to relax her hands. It didn't work. "A little. I'll be fine once we're up in the air. Something like ninety percent of all plane crashes happen during takeoff and landing. Bad things don't happen once the plane is in the air." The sky always held Hazel's fears. She'd been flying since she was a child but had never been comfortable with it. Aspen used to tease her and tell her all the different ways a plane could crash.

Which is why she always sat next to Rowan when they flew. He would rattle on about his stupid video games. She never had any idea what he was talking about, but it distracted her from the idea that they might crash. Her heart tightened. He might not ever be able to help her with that again.

"I guess that makes sense. I've never been on a plane before."

Hazel snorted. "Really. You live in Hawaii, and you've never been on a plane? That's hard to believe. Surely you've flown to one of the other islands."

He didn't reply and looked out the window. Had she offended him? Before she could stop herself, she forged on. She couldn't help it. Beautiful boys were her weakness.

"What's your name?"

His eyes met hers again, and her insides buzzed.

"Val."

"Why are you heading to the mainland?" The plane pushed away from the gate, and she clenched the armrests tighter, the plastic digging into her palms. She had to take deep breaths and inhale the stale airplane air, but she wanted to continue this conversation.

"I'm going to see my father. I haven't seen him since I was a young child. What about you? Why are you flying north?"

"My brother has gone missing. I'm going to look for him."

"That's awful. What happened?" Val placed his hand on top of hers. She wanted to shake it off, but she didn't want to let go of the armrest.

"They think a dragon got him."

Val's eyebrows raised. "You mean the one in Yellowstone?"

"That's what they're saying, but I don't think so. Rowan doesn't go outside. It's more likely a friend played a trick on him, and he's on a train to Canada or something." At least that is what she hoped. She'd been trying to come up with every possibility so she didn't have to think about him being dead. She kept her gaze locked on the seat in front of her as the plane taxied out to the runway. This was the worst part of flying.

A balding man brushed past her, and a flight attendant intercepted him.

"Sir, the fasten seatbelt sign is on. You need to take your seat." Her voice was clipped and irritated. The kind that mothers use when they've told a child something for the thousandth time.

"I was supposed to be bumped up to first class." He held up his ticket, but the flight attendant didn't even look at it.

"As you can see, this is a completely full flight. I'm afraid there weren't any seats to bump you up to."

The man pointed at Hazel. "She got on the plane late. Are you sure she paid for a first class ticket?"

"Sir, we can work this out after the plane takes off. I really need you to take your seat."

"No. I paid for an upgrade, and I want it. I was told I had to sit back in coach until they figured out which seat was empty. That seat was empty until two minutes ago."

Hazel's shoulders dropped. She knew this was too good to be true.

Val leaned over Hazel. He smelled like the sea, and Hazel had to resist the urge to stick her nose in his neck.

"I'm sorry. I don't mean to interrupt, but I couldn't help but hear your conversation. Hazel and I are traveling together. She is scared of flying so she always waits until the last minute to get on the plane. This was her seat."

The man glowered at him. "Oh yeah, prove it."

The flight attendant pointed to the coach section. "Sir, if you don't go and sit down, we'll be forced to turn this plane around, and you won't be going to San Francisco at all."

The balding man glared at Hazel again and then stomped back to his seat.

Hazel waited until the flight attendant was out of earshot. "Thank you. You didn't have to do that."

He shrugged. "I did it for my benefit, not yours. Who wants to sit next to a grump like that the entire flight?"

Hazel couldn't help herself and laughed. "Who indeed?"

He settled back but kept his gaze on her. "My father lives near Yellowstone. Where does your family live?"

"Gardiner."

"Really? That's where I'm heading." He rubbed his chin, and Hazel stared at his lips again.

The plane turned onto the main runway, and Hazel squeezed her eyes shut. She really hated flying. She gripped the armrests again.

"You know, I read that statistically you have a greater chance of dying in a car accident than an airplane crash."

Hazel nodded without opening her eyes. She spoke through clenched teeth. "I know. The fear is totally irrational, but it doesn't change the fact that I'm terrified. I'll be okay in a few minutes."

The plane picked up speed. She grasped the armrest tighter. Val put his hand over hers again, and she nearly opened her eyes. But he didn't stop there.

He dug his soft fingers underneath her palm and flipped her hand over, intertwining his fingers with hers. His hand was dry against her clammy one. Hazel tried to still her racing heart.

The wheels left the ground, and Hazel crushed his hand. For some reason, it was more satisfying than the armrest. She opened her eyes a sliver and looked at him staring out the window. His profile was just as nice to look at. After a few more minutes, the plane leveled off and she relaxed. She let go of the armrest and pulled her hand out of Val's, wiping her palms on her jeans.

"Thank you," she said and gave him a coy smile.

His face lit up, and he turned in his seat. "You're welcome. It helped? I also read that physical touch is always more reassuring than inanimate objects. Though I'm surprised you didn't break my hand." He flexed his hand.

Hazel grimaced. "Sorry."

She pointed to the TV on the back of the seat in front of him. "Are you going to watch a movie?"

He shook his head. "I'd rather talk to you."

Hazel's stomach flip-flopped. She wasn't sure what to make of him. He was gorgeous and smooth. Was he looking for an easy pick up, or was he genuinely interested? Only one way to find out.

"I have a boyfriend," she blurted. It was true. Sort of.

"I'd still like to talk to you, if that's okay."

Phew, he was only looking for someone to flirt with on the plane. That she could handle. Encourage, even.

Hazel leaned back but slid her foot forward so it was touching his. He didn't move. That was a good sign.

"I guess," she responded.

"How long have you been together?"

She watched his lips as he spoke. They looked soft. And she had no idea what he said.

"What?"

"Your boyfriend, how long have you two been together?"

"Oh, three months. I think." She dropped her eyes. There was no way she could look at him and concentrate on what he said with the sun outside the window reflecting off his hair.

"Three months isn't very long."

Especially when you considered that they had an open relationship. But she wasn't about to tell this beautiful man that. She played with the neckline of her shirt, mostly out of habit, not because she was trying to get him to look. Though she wouldn't mind. She needed to deflect the attention off herself.

"How come you haven't seen your father since you were young?" Hazel asked.

Val frowned, and even that looked sexy. She forced herself to look into his eyes as he spoke. "He was sent to the mainland because he got in some trouble, and he wasn't allowed to come back. Until a few weeks ago, I thought he was dead."

"Is he in jail?" She leaned closer to him, genuinely interested. She loved scandal and mysteries. Well, until it involved her family. Damn. She was thinking about Rowan again. Maybe *he* was in jail or something, and no one knew. It would be better than thinking he froze to death in the forests of Yellowstone. Or eaten by a dragon. But Hazel tried not to think of that possibility.

Val shook his head. "But he's not allowed to leave Montana. Well, now he could. But he's very sick."

Hazel's stomach dropped. She hated thinking about death. "I'm sorry to hear that. How much longer does he have?"

Val creased his eyebrows. "What do you mean?"

"He's dying, right? How long will you have with him?"

"He's sick, but he's not dying."

"Okay, sorry. I just assumed." Now she felt like an idiot.

"It's okay." He adjusted his legs and moved his foot away from hers. He took the book in lap and shoved it in seat pocket. A flight attendant handed them a menu. Val looked at his.

Hazel glanced at her menu for just a few seconds then handed it back to the flight attendant. "I'll have the chicken."

"And to drink?"

"A Sprite, please."

Val gave back his menu as well. "I'll have the same, but I'd like orange juice instead of Sprite."

The flight attendant disappeared.

"Why are you in Hawaii?" Val asked.

"I'm going to school. I got a scholarship, and I like to surf, so I jumped on it," Hazel responded. That, and she was running from Paul, who thought senior year would be a good time to propose. She had planned to stay close to home, but as soon as he popped the question, she accepted the scholarship to U of H and left four months later. Because really, who proposes to a girl that has explicitly told them she didn't want to commit to anyone?

"What school do you go to?" She wanted to keep him talking.

"I don't. Not yet, anyway. I used to watch the surfers. Never went in the water myself though."

"Why?"

"I can't swim."

Hazel frowned. "You live in Hawaii, and you can't swim? That sounds like torture."

"Yeah, sort of. But it's not so bad. I've waded in a little bit. Mostly I spend my time near the volcanoes."

Hazel couldn't help but be fascinated by him. He lived in Hawaii but had never been on a plane or swimming. That was like being a vegetarian in Texas.

"I saw the active volcanoes a few months ago when my sister came to visit. Not many people live on the Big Island. Too many dragons."

"I like the dragons."

Hazel rolled her eyes. "You'll like my sister. She's totally in love with them."

"You make it sound like I'll be meeting her." He watched her expectantly.

Hazel blushed. Not the response she was looking for from him. He was nice to talk to on the plane, but she didn't want to see him again. He would be too much of a distraction from helping find Rowan.

"Probably not. But really, what is there to like about dragons? They're a nuisance at best and dangerous at the worst. They serve no practical purpose. All they do is prevent us from enjoying some of the most beautiful places on earth."

He frowned. "I think they add to the beauty. People avoid the places because of an irrational fear. You're scared of flying, and yet here you are. Look at this gorgeous view." He pointed out the window.

Hazel snorted. "You'd see a lot more people visit the national parks if there were no dragons."

"Are you proposing killing all of them?"

"Of course not. I'm just saying I don't like them."

He crossed his arms and looked outside. Great, she'd made him mad. He took her mind off other things, like her brother.

The fasten seatbelt sign went off, and Hazel jumped up and raced for the bathroom. Maybe she'd regain her dignity in there.

CHAPTER 2

V AL LOOKED OUT the window and sighed. She had
been so promising. Theo told him his primary job as a new
king was finding a queen. So he looked everywhere for her.
Hazel was the first woman he spoke to that he thought he might actually be able to stomach spending the rest of his life with.

Part of him just wanted to find her so he could learn the rest of his
duties. He liked Hazel. He shook his head at the thought of bringing
her to the council and informing them that he'd found his queen. But
there was one problem. She hated dragons. Oh well, he was told he'd
have help finding his queen once he reached the mainland.

He still couldn't quite believe he was on plane heading there. As
a king. Until it happened, he thought it was impossible. Only royal
dragons became kings. Val was a fire dragon.

But exactly ten days ago, Val had been flying back from Lanai after visiting one of the exiled dragons with his uncle Rojo when it happened. The air was cool high up in the clouds. He felt no physical change.

Valentine, please don't panic, but you've changed. Rojo was calm. He was always calm.

Val laughed. *I'm always changing.*

No, you don't understand. Your scales, they've changed.

My scales?

Yes, your scales.

Val twisted his head around and looked at his flank. It was pitch black. Val dropped a few feet as he turned around the other way. Everything he could see of his body was black.

How is this possible? Maybe it's just a trick of the light. Am I sick?

I don't know, but we should go to the elders. They will know what to do.

Val's mind had spun as he thought of all the possibilities. There was only one black dragon, and he was always a royal dragon. The king. In fact, they just crowned a new king. His name was Obsidian. Val was a fire dragon. This was not possible. Was he sick? Would he die like his parents? No one ever told him how they died.

Rojo changed direction and flew to Eros's home, since Eros was the leader of their clan and council representative. If he was on the mainland, they could go see the other two elders who lived in caves close by. Eros's cave was dark, so they immediately went to Hoa's cave.

She let out a small flame when she saw him.

Your Majesty, she said, lowering her head. Val's insides went cold. This was impossible.

No, it's just me. Valentine. We don't know what happened.

She raised her head and studied him. *We need Eros, but he's at the council. I'll send an eagle.*

What's wrong with me?

I don't know. Go home, and we'll wait until we hear from Eros.

Val waited. For nearly forty-eight hours. When Eros arrived, he brought a tall gold royal dragon with him named Theo, who studied Val for a few minutes before speaking.

Have you ever heard of the Legend of the Three Kings?

Of course, it was one of my favorite stories as a young dragon. Three kings will rise up and kill the Evil Witch of the North.

Very good. But the legend is a prophecy. And you are the beginning of its fulfillment.

Val shuffled back a few steps, trying to make sense of what Theo said.

Are you saying I'm a king? Val's muscled tensed.

Yes. One of three. The third hasn't been identified yet.

But I'm not of the royal race. Something about this had to make sense. What was he missing?

Eros spoke up. *We've always suspected that the three kings would come from different races.*

But I'm not a leader. He was a low-ranking dragon. The fire dragons were laid back, none really aspired to leadership. They were peaceful, and their elders rarely had to deal with issues. Val figured he'd eventually find a mate and live out his years on the island. Now that dream was gone.

Theo shook his head. *You will be a leader now. We'll be here for a week or so, and then we'll head back to Montana. I can only teach you so much. Obsidian, the first king, will have to teach you the rest.*

Val didn't know what to think, what to feel. The only thing he could do was move forward.

What do we do first?

Let's give you a human form.

And so it began. A week and a half of stumbling around on two legs. Reading books. Watching movies. Interacting with humans.

The person behind him kicked his seat, and Val was brought back to the present. Secretly, Val was thrilled with the fact that he got to be a human. It was the only good thing that came out of becoming king. He never thought humanity was a possibility since only royal dragons got to be humans. His aunt and uncle had never understood his fascination with humans, but he'd spent most of his free time watching them. He wondered if he'd ever seen Hazel before. Probably. Surfing was one of his favorite things to watch.

He shook his head. He couldn't think about her. He had less than six months to find a mate, and she obviously wasn't going to work.

Instead, he thought of the news that had really rocked his world. Last night, while they were eating dinner, Theo asked him if he'd ever head of Damien.

"That was the name of my father. He's dead." Val took a bite of his cheeseburger. He wasn't sure he could ever go back to eating as a dragon again. Human food was incredible.

"He's not dead."

Val spewed bits of burger and cheese. "Excuse me?"

"He lives with the royal dragons, and he can't wait to meet you."

Val's appetite disappeared. "Why did no one tell me?"

Theo had shrugged. "I don't know his story. I know he's not allowed to leave Yellowstone though."

Val knew he should be more focused on how to become a real king, not just a dragon that looked like one. But he couldn't stop thinking about his father. Did that mean his mother was alive too?

A man plopped himself down in the seat where Hazel should be. Val met his eyes. It was the man who had been arguing about Hazel's seat.

"Excuse me, sir, I think you have the wrong seat." Val wanted Hazel sitting there even if she didn't like dragons.

"Nope, don't think I do." The man had a receding hairline, wore glasses, and had a blazer over a blue button down. He reached into his inside pocket and started pulling something out.

Hazel appeared, eyes blazing. "You're in my seat." She crossed her arms and tapped her foot.

The man withdrew his empty hand. "No, sweetie, this is my seat. You can go back and sit in 27E. Nice middle seat in coach. Go on." He waved toward the back.

The flight attendant hurried to them. "Sir, you are disturbing the passengers. You must go back to your seat. If you don't leave, the police will arrest you when we arrive in San Francisco."

The man glared at all of them as he got up and moved out of the first class section.

"I'm sorry about him. If he bothers you again, make sure you alert us right away. Can I get you two anything?"

Hazel settled back in her seat. "I'm fine, thanks though."

"Are you sure? We just warmed up some cookies. We were waiting for them to cool, but I can bring them to you now if you want."

"Chocolate chip?" Hazel asked. Val wondered what chocolate chip tasted like. He couldn't wait to find out.

The flight attendant smiled. "Of course."

"Not going to turn that down." Hazel had a grin on her face, and once again Val regretted the fact that she didn't like dragons.

"I'll be right back," the flight attendant said and disappeared into the galley.

"Geesh, he doesn't know how to take a hint, does he?" Hazel asked.

Val gave her a small smile and looked out the window again, even though there wasn't much to see other than clouds. He wanted to fly to Montana as a dragon, but Theo told him he had to get used to the way humans did things, and planes were part of the equation. Theo was supposed to be sitting in the seat next to him, but had sent him a message a few minutes before boarding that he'd meet Val on the mainland.

"I'm sorry," Hazel said, her voice gentle.

Val turned to face her, and her beauty struck him. He'd watched a lot of humans over the years, and for some reason she was more attractive to him than most. It was the combination of her wide green eyes and jet black hair. Her sun-kissed skin seemed to sparkle. She continued to speak but kept her gaze lowered.

"I didn't mean to upset you. I don't like dragons. Can we forget about that and talk about something else? It's what my sister and I do. We usually just avoid the subject of dragons."

He supposed talking couldn't hurt. Maybe then he could meet her sister who liked dragons. Theo seemed to think that finding a queen was the most important job Val had as a king.

"Sure." He settled back and stretched his arms up. The flight attendant came back with the cookies and handed them each one. Hazel took a bite of hers and moaned.

"That good?" Val asked.

"Yes. And if you don't eat that, I'm going to finish it for you."

Val tried his and was surprised by the sweetness. They were good, though Hazel seemed to enjoy hers more than he did his.

After Hazel finished her cookie, she eyed him carefully. "How come you never learned how to swim?" Her eyes danced with curiosity.

Val wasn't sure how to answer that. He knew a lot about humans because he'd spent so much time observing them. He'd even hid out in the forests behind people camping and listened to their conversations. He probably had a better grasp of humans than the royal dragons, but he had no idea what she expected him to say. He'd learned it was better to give an answer that was expected, otherwise they got suspicious.

He and Theo had spent a good deal of time inventing a human back-story for him, and it served his purposes now.

"I grew up believing both my mother and father were dead. My aunt and uncle told me they died in an accident on the water. I guess I was just scared. An irrational fear." He gave her what he hoped was an encouraging smile, and she leaned even closer to him. He wasn't sure what she was up to, but he was thinking thoughts he shouldn't, like what those lips would taste like and if the scent of jasmine coming from her hair would smell even stronger if he were to embrace her. The desire to touch her was almost overwhelming.

"Tell me more about your parents."

He sucked in a breath. "Why are so you curious about my parents?"

"I don't know. I like mysteries, and this is a mystery. You already told me your father is alive, so if they didn't die on the water, what happened?"

He'd really hoped to learn about her, not tell her his life story. Most humans liked to talk about themselves more than listening to someone else. The flight attendant interrupted their conversation by coming around giving everyone their meals. She spoke with her coworker who was serving the row in front of them.

"I still haven't heard from my sister in Alaska. I'm worried sick."

"Did she live in the town that had the avalanche?"

"No, one town over from the fire. But I heard buildings all over Alaska are catching fire."

"What happened in Alaska?" Val asked Hazel.

"Uh, Alaska? Where have you been? It's been on the news all week. Unexplained avalanches everywhere. One small town was completely buried. Then a huge fog moved into another town on the coast, and when the fog disappeared, buildings all over were in flames. It started a few days ago. Then yesterday, a cruise ship literally capsized. Everyone died. No one can explain it," Hazel replied.

"That sounds awful," said Val.

"It is. Some people are speculating that it's the dragons up north. It's like they've declared war on us or something. But no one has reported seeing one."

War. He wondered if she was right. Theo had told him that the war would begin soon and that it would be the arctic dragons against the rest of them. And he was supposed to stand beside Obsidian and the third king, and the three would lead everyone into battle.

Hazel tapped his knuckles. "Your parents. What happened?"

He squeezed his eyes shut and opened them again. Glad to have the distraction.

"I don't actually know what happened. It's part of the reason I'm going to the mainland. To find out. I don't know why my father had to go to Montana and why I couldn't go with him. Also, I want to know how my mother died."

That was absolutely the truth, and he planned on getting that answer out of his father before he did anything else, even though he had new responsibilities as a dragon king. He frowned. He was never supposed to be king. Hell, he wasn't even slated for leadership among the fire dragons. How was he going to do this?

"You okay?" Hazel asked, studying him.

He squirmed. "I'm fine, why do you ask?"

"Because you look like you are about to throw up."

"I'm just worried. What if I don't like the answers I get when I meet my father for the first time?" He liked talking to her. He didn't know why he felt the need to say so much. She was comfortable. A lot more than Theo had been. He rubbed his forehead.

"You probably won't. But you'll process through it and move on. We all do. If you want, after you talk to him, you can call me to process. I'm a good listener."

"Why do you care?" This girl was constantly surprising him

She shrugged. "I told you. Mystery. I like answers. My family tells me I'm too nosy for my own good. I can't stand not knowing the end to stories."

"So you don't care about my feelings, just satisfying your own curiosity?" He raised his eyebrows at her.

She laughed and put her hand on his. "Sorry. I get caught up in the answers and forget about the human side of things."

He looked down at their hands, enjoying her touch.

"Fine. I'll tell you, but not over the phone. You'll have to come to dinner with me."

"I told you I have a boyfriend." She blushed.

"I'm calling bullshit. I've seen girls with boyfriends, and you don't act like it at all." Maybe she did have a boyfriend, but if so, she wasn't in love with him. He used to watch couples on the island, and he got good at identifying those that were in love and those that were just messing around with each other. Her attitude told him all he needed to know.

She pushed her dark hair behind her ears. "No, I really do have a boyfriend, but we're in an open relationship."

"What does that mean?"

"That we can date other people. It's pretty casual. I don't really do commitment."

"Why don't you do commitment? That's the best part of relationships."

"Because that's the easiest way to get your heart crushed. It happened to me, and I'm not really interested in recreating the experience."

"You mean to tell me that you would give up all the good parts of your relationship just because of one bad experience?"

"Absolutely. If I could go back and erase that entire summer, I would. I'm sure my sister would too. We call that the summer of hell and don't talk about it much. She finally moved on though. I never will because the heartache isn't worth the rest of it."

Hazel's hand was still resting on his. It felt warm and nice, and he'd be lying if he said he wasn't starting to develop feelings for this girl. He thought about flipping his hand over so he could hold hers but didn't want to spook her. He leaned forward.

"I told you what I know about my father. I want to hear about this summer of hell."

Hazel hesitated, and Val had the irresistible urge to kiss her. He'd never kissed anyone before, but he'd seen it a lot. It always seemed so intimate to him though. Something that was done in private, not in an airplane surrounded by people.

She sighed and turned in her seat so one knee was brought up. She tucked her foot under her other leg. "I guess I owe you one. My parents are park rangers. One summer they did a stint in California. In spite of growing up in the parks, I'm not all that crazy about mountains and trees. I like the water better. I liked living in the Everglades a helluva lot more than I liked Yellowstone, so when they went to Yosemite, I was ecstatic to be closer to the ocean. But it's still a three to four-hour drive to a beach. My aunt lives in San Francisco, so she let me stay whenever I wanted. I had never surfed before, and I met this guy who offered to teach me.

"His name was Teddy, and he was a few years older. I never found out how much older because he was vague about his age. He taught me how to surf, and I fell hard. For two glorious months we were inseparable. I still remember how his lips felt on mine. No one could match his kisses." Her eyes glazed over a little, and he finally understood what jealousy felt like. Val thought it was odd that she was so open about it. She seemed almost wistful.

"One weekend, I had to go to Yosemite to spend some time with my family, and when I got back to the beach, he was gone. Disappeared. He blocked my calls and texts. Someone told me he moved to L.A."

The kind of behavior she was talking about seemed abhorrent to Val. Love was not something that was trifled with or made light of. Teddy needed his head examined.

"The worst part is I have no idea what happened. One minute we were happy, and the next he was just gone. Took my heart with him too."

"Sounds like someone needs to give your heart back to you."

"Or not. The rest of that summer was awful. My sister and I holed up and ate a lot of ice cream. I enjoy my life now. It's more fun without commitment. No worries about doing the wrong thing or hurting someone. I'm upfront with anyone I get involved with." She brushed her hair over her shoulder.

"Sounds lonely."

"Not really. I never lack company."

Of course she didn't. With those bright knowing eyes and smile to die for, she was gorgeous. He couldn't help himself. He leaned forward and traced a finger along her jaw. "That's because you are beautiful and interesting. I imagine you've hurt more than your fair share of men."

She batted her eyes. "I doubt that's true. But thank you."

She looked away from him, and he wondered what she was thinking. If he was a canyon dragon, he could tell, but he wasn't. He was a fire dragon. His gift was a bit useless around humans. Fire dragons were the reason all the rest could breathe fire. They were also pretty charming, but he didn't want to win Hazel over with his charm. He wanted her to genuinely like him. Why, he didn't know. She would never agree to be a dragon queen. Which was too bad. He'd been talking to women all week, wondering who would be suitable. He hadn't liked any of them. Now he'd be comparing everyone to her.

"What are you thinking about?" he finally asked when the silence stretched for too long.

She looked at him and opened her mouth like she was about to say something, but then pulled her bag out from under the seat in front of her.

She wouldn't meet his eyes. "This plane ride has been very unexpected. I think I'll watch a movie now. It's been a nice conversation." It all came out in a rush, like she wanted to stay the words before she forgot them.

Panic bloomed in his chest. She was going to shut him out.

"No, wait. I'm sorry. I don't know what I said, but I'd like to keep talking to you. I'll avoid the topic of your beauty if that helps."

She laughed, settled her bag in her lap, and smiled at him.

"Surfers are the most romantic guys on the block, and I've hooked up with my fair share of them. Every single one tells me I'm beautiful. But there was something about the way you said it. It was like you didn't expect anything from me." She creased her eyebrows.

He caught her eye. "Why would I have any expectations?"

She held his gaze for a few seconds and then broke away and dug around in her backpack. "That's the problem. If you weren't heading to the same place I was, I would probably indulge this. It's easier than thinking about my brother. But Gardiner is a small town, and we'll run into each other. You seem like a really nice guy, but I don't have time for a fling while I'm home." She gave a small smile and patted his hand.

She pulled out a pair of headphones and shoved the bag underneath the seat. He looked at the screen in front of him with their flight information. Four hours left.

He thought about kissing her, but that might be going a bit too far. Instead, he grabbed her hand.

"I have no expectations beyond this plane. There are four hours left. Can we have a four-hour, uh, fling as you called it?" He had no earthly idea what he was doing. This wasn't like him. At all.

CHAPTER 3

H AZEL LOOKED DOWN at the hand holding hers. She really liked this guy. Too much. She hadn't felt like this since Teddy. This was like one of those cheesy teen romance novels. The instalove that never made any sense. Instalove? What was she thinking? He was attractive, and she enjoyed talking to him. Love. Ha!

She didn't really want to end their conversation, but he was too real. A four-hour fling wasn't exactly what she had in mind when she thought about him. But it wouldn't be a horrible thing.

"You just want to join the mile-high club." She grinned at him.

He creased his eyebrows. "What's that?"

She didn't let go of his hand. "If you don't know, I'm not telling you. You don't seem to know much about relationships."

"My aunt and uncle kept me pretty sheltered. The only other people I knew were on the island."

He was so damned genuine. If she tried to watch a movie, she'd just be thinking about him. "Okay, but as soon as we get off this plane, we're done. Is that fair?"

He nodded.

Hazel had never had a flight go so fast. He talked about the island he loved, and she told him of her adventures. She avoided the topic of her family because she didn't want to think about Rowan. Val was smooth and charming but nice. Maybe she should stop dating surfer boys.

He didn't try to make any moves except to hold her hand. She supposed it would be awkward on the plane, but she hoped to get a kiss out of this before it was over.

Hazel was surprised when the fasten seatbelt sign came on again.

The captain announced they were starting their descent. Hazel gripped Val's hand. He chuckled.

"Hey, we're going to be okay."

She nodded, her words lost now. They still had twenty minutes until things got really scary. Someone bumped into her seat, and she looked up and saw the man who kept trying to steal her seat.

He leaned over her, syringe in hand. It took Hazel only a fraction of second to see that he was heading straight for Val. Hazel acted instinctively and hit the man's hand. The syringe went flying, and the man growled at her. Hazel's heart raced as she tried to comprehend what was going on.

"Stupid girl. I knew you were going to ruin this." He grabbed Val by the collar, but before he could do anything else, two large men descended on the man and tackled him to the ground. Hazel felt instant relief flood through her. In seconds, one man had him in handcuffs, and the other turned to Hazel.

"We're air marshals. Are you okay?"

"Yeah," she said, but her pulse sounded loud in her ears.

Val was pale, but seemed no worse for wear.

"Where's the syringe? We saw him pull one out," one of the air marshals asked.

Hazel thought for a second. "I don't know. It went flying."

Hazel stood and looked in the direction she saw it go, scared she might see it stuck in someone's neck. It was on the floor next to the first row. A woman sat there watching the whole scene. Her eyes were wide, and her breath was coming in rapid bursts. "It nicked me," she said pointing to her arm.

The air marshal holding the man down pushed his knee into the man's back. "What was in the syringe?"

"Not telling."

"Yes, you will," the air marshal said. He pulled on one of the man's fingers and bent it back. "Normal rules don't apply up here. If that was deadly, we need to know."

"Ow, ow, ow. Stop. Okay, I'll tell you. It's potassium cyanide."

The air marshal looked at the woman in the front. "You'll be fine if it only nicked you. If you start feeling dizzy, alert one of the flight attendants." The other air marshal stepped over the man and picked up the syringe. Then the first marshal stood the man up and walked him toward the front. When the man got close enough to the second air marshal, he struggled and forced his arm onto the syringe so that it plunged right into his bicep. Then he fell limp.

The air marshals dragged him to the forward galley.

"Do you think he's dead?" Hazel asked. She shivered and tried to steady her breathing. They couldn't see the marshals or the man anymore, but flight attendants were rushing about calming scared passengers. Since the whole thing took place in first class, most of the passengers behind the curtain had no idea what happened. The marshals were talking, but they were too far away from them to hear what was said.

Val face paled. "Why do you think he wanted me dead? He was coming straight for me."

A few minutes later, one of the air marshals appeared at their side and stared hard at Val. "Have you ever seen that man before?"

"No. I have no idea why he would do that."

"Is he dead?" Hazel interrupted, needing to know. If she hadn't stopped the man, what would he have done to Val?

"Yes. That was quick thinking. He owes you one." The marshal said, pointing to Val.

The marshal gave Val a card and asked for his number, then went back up to the front.

Val looked at her with an ashen face. "No one has tried to kill me before."

"He was probably crazy." She grabbed his hand. "He's dead now, so there's nothing else to worry about."

The plane started to descend, and she squeezed his hand.

"What time is your next flight?" he asked.

"Two," she whispered.

He nodded. "Okay, that means we'll be on that plane together. I'll get our seats switched around so you can sit next to me in that flight as well. That way I can hold your hand."

She squeezed her eyes shut. "Sounds good," she squeaked. She couldn't get anything else out. This was the worst part of the plane ride.

"We'll have a couple of hours. Would you like to get lunch with me in the airport?"

She took a couple of deep breaths. "Yeah. That would be nice."

He continued to talk to her, and she responded with one-word answers. She didn't open her eyes until she felt the wheels touch the ground. Then she relaxed her grip and breathed normally.

"Thanks. It helped to have you talk to me."

"Maybe we'll get lucky and have the same flight back to Hawaii."

"That would be quite the coincidence. Do you know when you're going back?"

He shook his head. "No. I want to see how things go with my dad first. What about you?"

"It all depends on how fast we find my brother. He's been missing for a week, but my parents waited until now to tell me. I'm a little peeved." She still had no idea why they waited so long to tell her. She'd get to the bottom of that when she got home.

They rolled their bags out into the terminal and headed to the food court.

"What do you like?" she asked.

"I'm not sure what's good. We didn't have all these choices on the Big Island."

"Five Guys is good. Do you like burgers?" Five Guys was her favorite, and after the exciting flight they just had, she needed comfort food.

"Yeah, I do. Let's try that."

They ordered their food, and five minutes later she watched him scarf down his fries. She found it weird he was so sheltered. "How old are you?"

"Nineteen." He dug into his burger.

"And until now, you never even left the Big Island?"

He chewed and swallowed. "Occasionally we'd visit other islands."

"But you'd never been on a plane." She ate a couple of fries.

"My aunt refused to fly. She was more scared than you." He grinned. "We took boats. But again, I had a rather strange upbringing. My aunt homeschooled me, and we didn't venture out past our neighborhood except on rare occasions. I probably would've left sooner, but I didn't know any better."

"Aside from not knowing about different restaurants and things, you're not all that weird. Most kids who grow up in your situation would be pretty odd."

"Glad you think I'm acceptable."

She flushed. "That's not what I meant. I just mean you're just not as naïve as I expected."

CHAPTER 4

THE ASSASSINATION ATTEMPT bothered Val. He wanted to talk to Hazel about it, but he couldn't without arousing suspicion—because all the possible reasons someone would want him dead had to do with dragons. He thought it might have something to do with the fact that he was the new king. Obsidian could help him figure this all out.

For the time being, Hazel was a welcome distraction. Val couldn't get enough of this girl. Even though he promised he wouldn't look her up once they got to Montana, he had no intention of keeping that promise. They ate their lunch and made their way to the gate. He left her to watch the bags and paid for her to upgrade to first class and sit next to him.

Hazel seemed pretty awed by his ability to do so, but he didn't really understand why. After he took a human form, Theo gave him a passport, driver's license, and a few credit cards with no limits. Though Theo did say that Val probably shouldn't buy a Maserati.

She looked at her ticket. "You've spoiled me with this first class stuff. I'm not looking forward to flying back in coach."

"If you're on my flight back, I'll bump you up."

Her smile fell. "You know I've totally enjoyed talking to you. But I'm serious about not pursuing this after we land. I have to find my brother."

"I know."

They boarded the plane, and once again he lost all the feeling in his hand with her death grip. Unfortunately, this flight was much shorter.

"What's your real name?" she asked.

"What?"

"Val has to be short for something. What's your real name?"

"Valentine."

She cocked her head in surprise, then giggled. "That's romantic."

He shrugged. He'd never thought much of his name. He supposed his mother gave it to him, but he didn't know. That was one of the thousand questions he'd ask his father. He'd be just as busy as she would be once they got to their destination, but all he wanted was to be with her.

"Do you have any nicknames?" he asked.

"Yeah, my family calls me Sissy. They've never called me anything else. My sister and brother are only eleven months younger than me."

"I like Hazel better."

"Me too, but I don't mind. It's just my family."

The captain came on the intercom again and announced they would be landing soon. Val wasn't ready for this to be over. Hazel buckled her seatbelt with shaking hands.

He'd find her when the plane ride was over. He had to. Hopefully she was right and Gardiner was a small town. Hazel was already gripping his hand tightly.

The captain made the announcement to prepare for landing. Val only had a few more minutes with the beautiful girl, and he planned on making the best of it.

"Hazel," he said. She didn't respond. He moved her chin so she was facing him, but her eyes were squeezed shut. "Hazel, look at me."

She peeked at him, and he smiled. Then he brought his face toward hers and kissed her. At first, she didn't react, her face tight from nerves, but then he felt all the tension leave her body, and her hand relaxed in his. She returned the kiss eagerly. Her hands wove into his hair and held his face against hers. He'd never felt so alive.

CHAPTER 5

HAZEL FORGOT WHERE she was. Space and time disappeared. This kiss was better than any she'd ever experienced. He tasted sweet like the sugar cookies at Christmas time. The wheels touched the ground, and Hazel broke the kiss but didn't move her face away from Val's. He rested his forehead on hers. She wondered if it was as good for him as it was for her. There was something about him that she couldn't explain. She felt that if she stayed with him forever, she'd never have to worry about anything ever again.

Her ankle burned, and she jerked away. That was weird. It felt like a jellyfish brushed up against her skin.

"This has been fun," she said, pulling away, not wanting to let on how much that kiss rattled her. She had to focus on her brother and couldn't let anyone distract her. She rubbed at her ankle. The burning subsided.

He gave her a half smile, and she nearly reached up and kissed him again. What the hell was wrong with her?

"That's one way to put it," Val said, his lips pursed.

He seemed like he wanted to ask her something, and she hoped against hope that it was for her number. She'd told him they couldn't see each other after the flight, but she wanted nothing more than to kiss him again.

"Penny for your thoughts?" she asked, looking past him to the dark sky out his window.

He shook his head and clenched his fists.

The flight attendant opened the door, and Hazel grabbed her bag from under the seat in front of her. She hesitated for a half second, almost asking for his number.

"Maybe I'll see you around," Val said, without looking at her. Maybe the kiss hadn't been as good for him as it had been for her. Rejection stung. Ah well. She shouldn't be thinking about him anyway.

"Maybe," she said, ignoring her racing heart as she escaped down the jetway. A tinge of sadness pricked her heart. Even in the jetway the frigid air of Idaho was already seeping into her bones. She felt a sense of loss. But maybe it was just the cold. She took a deep breath. She couldn't think like this. She had another boy to find.

As long as he hadn't already frozen to death.

CHAPTER 6

HAZEL'S DAD MET her as she walked into the area with the baggage carousels. People swarmed around them as he gave her a big hug. He smelled of sweat and pine, much like he always did, but when she pulled away, she saw the weariness on his face. He'd always been pretty laid back. It was rare to see him stressed out.

"Where are Mom and Aspen?" she asked, shrugging off her backpack and handing it to him.

"Out looking." He took the backpack, and she rolled her carry-on.

"Of course." Hazel's stomach twisted as she followed him to the door. His shoulders slouched, and his gait was slower than normal.

Hazel gasped when they stepped outside. The icy air hit her, burning her lungs. Rowan wouldn't survive in weather like this. Her dad threw the suitcase in the bed of the truck, and Hazel climbed up in, hissing when her legs hit the cold leather. Her wimpy sweats were no match for the sub-zero temps. She'd need to dig out her winter gear when they got home.

"What do they think happened?" Hazel asked when her dad shut his door.

"Honestly, no one is sure." He ran his hand through his hair. "He'd been doing so well. He was making friends and going out."

"Rowan?" Her brother had been a loner since they were young children. Her parents had worried about it, but she always just accepted that Rowan never left home. He'd helped her cover up her sneaking out on more than one occasion. Now she felt awful for taking advantage of him. But if his behavior had changed recently, maybe that meant they were looking at his disappearance wrong.

"Do you think his new friends had anything to do with it?" Hazel wondered what had changed in his life.

"No. They were all Aspen's friends. In the last few months they've been inseparable."

"Aspen and Rowan?" Now that was news. The last time she'd talked to Aspen she'd been lamenting the loss of Tori because of her new boyfriend. Hazel didn't like Tori anyway. Hazel should've kept up with Aspen more, but between school and hitting the waves, she didn't talk to her family very often.

"Surprised? So were we. But it was nice seeing him happy." Dad paused for a few seconds. "I'm afraid I'll never see that smile again." His voice cracked.

Hazel reached over and grasped his hand. "We'll find him. I'm sure of it."

He turned on the windshield wipers as wet snow began to fall. "There have been several deaths over the last few months. That dragon. Even Aspen has admitted it's a possibility. Sis, I'm afraid he's dead."

"No way. Look, even if Rowan has been acting differently the last few months, he wouldn't go out in the woods. That's not like him at all."

"The dragon isn't just eating hikers. He got one boy just off the road. The military has come in. There's talk of taking out the dragons. Aspen is furious."

Hazel shook her head. Only Aspen would be more worried about the dragons than she was about her brother. Dragons were always Aspen's downfall. Hazel hated to think her sister was out fighting for dragon rights instead of looking for Rowan.

The rest of the drive went by in silence. Hazel didn't want to think about Rowan, so she stared out the window and thought of Val. The kiss. By the time they got home, it was nearly ten. Her mom's truck was in the driveway, but Aspen's jeep was missing.

She hugged her mom, who squeezed her tight. "I'm so glad you're here."

"Me too."

There were dark lines under her mother's eyes. Her dad sat down on the couch and hung his head. They both looked utterly exhausted.

"Have they been searching at night?" Hazel asked, sitting next to her mom.

"The first couple of nights we did. But between the cold and the dark, it's nearly impossible. We have a better shot at finding him in the daylight. Besides, we need to rest. Not that we've been sleeping well."

"Of course not. I'm going to go shower and hit the sack so I can get an early start tomorrow. I'd like to visit with Aspen first. Where is she?" Hazel wanted to find out what Aspen knew. She was smarter than all of them put together. If anyone knew about Rowan's disappearance, Aspen did.

"She spends most nights at Sid's. She and Rowan had been staying there before he disappeared because the park was shut down. I think it's easier for her to stay there than to come home."

Hazel's chest tightened. "Did she know I was coming?"

"Yeah. She said she would see you in the morning."

Hazel felt absurdly annoyed. It should be fine that she waited until morning to see Aspen, but maybe she was just feeling off because she wanted her whole family together.

Hazel half expected Rowan to be waiting on her bed when she opened the door. When he used to cover her ass when she snuck out, he never threatened to tell their mom and dad, but he did have a price. He wanted her to tell him stories of her adventures. So he was always waiting for her when she got home, and she'd regale him with her exploits. He was a fantastic listener, and they'd often lay awake for hours laughing at the trouble she could get in. She'd offered to take him with a few times, but he always turned her down. He said it was safer to live through her.

Now he was out on his own adventure. Hazel hoped he was having the time of his life. She imagined him off with his own friends, road tripping to Washington or something. She wanted him to be doing something stupid because that meant he wasn't dead.

She dumped her bag in her room and dug out a pair of thick sweats from her dresser. Then she opened another drawer and pulled out her long underwear. She'd hoped she would never have to wear those again. But she was glad her parents left her room intact even though she didn't come that often.

In the bathroom she stripped down quickly and stepped into the shower, hoping the hot water would warm her up. After she shampooed her hair, she grabbed her razor out of habit. When she leaned down to run the razor over her left calf, she saw a flash of black on her ankle.

What the hell?

She stretched out her foot. An intricate black tattoo encircled her ankle. She had a dolphin tattoo on her shoulder, but that was on purpose. This was new.

She turned off the water, her razor forgotten. She dressed quickly, her sweatshirt sticking to her wet skin, sat on the edge of the tub, rested her leg on her knee, and studied the beautiful tattoo. The pattern was a mixture of crisscrosses and loops, a couple of inches wide. In the middle of the loops were several words in a strange language. There was only one word she could read, and it made her blood run cold.

Valentine.

CHAPTER 7

VAL LOOKED UP at the enormous house and hesitated. Most of the humans in his area had small homes. This looked like it could house a hundred humans. It made him feel incredibly insignificant, which only added to his nerves.

He was about to meet Obsidian. The dragon king. Though Val knew he was a king as well, that reality hadn't quite hit him yet. He wondered if he'd ever feel like a real king, since he would always be the second king. He'd defer to Obsidian.

He wiped his palms on his jeans and knocked on the door. He couldn't stay out there much longer without his eyelids freezing together. He missed Hawaii already. Though he did like watching the snow fall. At home he would sometimes fly up to the tall peaks and play in the snow.

Obsidian opened the door. Even as a human, he looked kingly. He was tall with dark hair and piercing blue eyes.

Obsidian smiled wide and waved him inside. "Come on in."

Val dragged his suitcase into the house and gave Obsidian a small bow.

"Hello, Your Majesty."

Obsidian clapped him on the back and let out a laugh. "I should say the same thing to you. No need for formalities here or anywhere else for that matter. You're a king. You bow to no one. Also, call me Sid. Everyone else does."

Val took a deep breath and moved farther into the house as Sid shut the door behind him. Sid took his coat and hung it on a rack by the door that held several wool coats and had boots scattered around underneath it.

"Do you ever get used to it?" Val asked.

"What?" Obsidian replied, staring him straight in the eyes. It was difficult not be intimidated.

"Being king?" Val looked past Sid to the massive stairway that took up most of the foyer.

Sid shook his head. "Not yet. But I wasn't expecting to be a king either."

"But I thought all kings were trained." Val scratched at his chin. He was not expecting Sid to be like this. He wasn't sure what he expected, but not someone who openly admitted they didn't know what they were doing.

"Oh, I was. But I never thought it'd actually happen to me. But let's talk about that later. I'll let you get settled in for the night. We'll start training tomorrow. Did you have a nice flight?"

"I did, thank you." He should tell Obsidian about Hazel and the man who tried to kill him, but he was still a little unsure of his place.

They walked into a kitchen where a pretty blonde girl stood by the counter. She looked at him with bright green eyes that were eerily similar to Hazel's.

"Meet my queen," Obsidian said with a grin. He pulled her close and kissed her neck. She wiggled out of his grip and stuck her hand out. "Hi! I'm Aspen."

"Nice to meet you, I'm Val."

She seemed eager to meet him. He instantly liked her.

"Are you tired? We had a room made up for you." Aspen bounced around on her feet. Was she just as nervous at meeting him as he was of her? He'd never met a queen before. Or a king for that matter.

Val shrugged. "Not really. Hungry though."

Obsidian laughed and pointed to the stove. "None of us cook well. Skye did when she was here, but we haven't seen her since the testing. There's some fruit in the fridge. Help yourself. I'm going to put your bag in your room. I'll be back in a second."

Aspen opened the fridge, and Val stared at all the food. Bright green and red fruits. A carton with a white liquid. Some containers with who knows what inside of them. The airplane was easy; he just ate what was given to him. Before that Theo made all of his choices. From the clothes he wore to the movies he watched. There was hardly any time for him to get used to being human. Theo told him it would be easier if he just did as he was told.

Before he turned black, Val had never expected to even be in the presence of royalty, let alone be one of them, so he listened to Theo.

Then at the airport he let Hazel make decisions for him. His heart squeezed at the thought of her. That sparkle in her eye and the way she cocked her head when he took her by surprise. He wanted to have her here with him. He didn't think it was possible to feel so strongly for someone in such a short amount of time.

"What's good?" he finally asked Aspen.

"Still getting used to being a human, huh?" She pulled out a few pieces of fruit. "The apples and bananas are decent. Make sure you peel the banana though." She pulled the bright yellow skin off the fruit.

"Thank you."

They sat at the table. "How was your flight?"

He smiled. "Interesting."

"This must be weird for you, huh? Are you coping okay?" She leaned back in her chair as he took a bite of the banana. The texture was strange, but the flavor was sweet.

Val was surprised by her concern. "It is a little strange, but so far I've found it to be nice."

Obsidian came back with a tiny dragon in tow.

"Why didn't you wake me up?" The little dragon landed on the table with a crash and glared at Aspen. "I wanted to meet the new king." She was a rainbow of colors, from her green head to her yellow wings. Her body was a swirl of pink and purple. He'd never seen such a dragon. Then again, before a week ago, he'd only seen his own kind.

Sid shrugged. "I didn't mean to wake her up, but she heard me putting the bags away."

Aspen offered the tiny dragon a piece of banana, which she gobbled up. "I've been taught to never wake a sleeping dragon. Besides, he's tired and doesn't want to be bothered."

"Nonsense." The dragon bobbed her head up and down in front of him. "I'm Runa. Can you take me to see the ocean? I've been asking everyone for weeks, but no one will take me."

"No one is going to the ocean for a while. We've got too much going on," Aspen said with a roll of her eyes.

Runa stuck her tongue out at Aspen and settled on the table in front of Val. He wasn't sure what to make of her.

"What kind of dragon are you?" he asked.

"Underground and river." She studied him with yellow eyes.

"She never shuts up. Kind of makes me wish she wasn't river," Aspen said with a laugh.

"Hey," Runa started, but Aspen shoved another piece of banana in her mouth.

Obsidian sat down across from him. "As Aspen said, there's a lot going on. There's a war coming. We need to bring you up to speed on the prophecy and train you for battle. But the priority is finding you a queen."

"Already done." Val sat a little taller, glad he'd done something right. Maybe being a king wouldn't be so hard.

Obsidian creased his eyebrows. "How is that possible? She has to be a human."

"Oh, I know. Theo explained it to me. Then, I met a girl on the airplane."

Aspen laughed. "It's not quite that easy."

Val's confidence fell. He wasn't quite sure if he knew what he was doing. But he did know that Hazel had sealed herself to him, so it couldn't be that bad.

Runa popped her head up. "Is she pretty like Aspen? What color are her eyes?"

Val smiled at her. "She is pretty, and she has green eyes like Aspen. She lives here in Gardiner. Look."

He pulled off his shoes and peeled away his sock. Aspen looked down and then shot back up. "That says Hazel."

"Yeah. She's pretty amazing." Val thought briefly of the kiss and had to fight to keep a silly grin off his face.

"I have a sister named Hazel." Aspen's eyebrows creased.

Val didn't think much of her comment. "Lots of Hazels in the world, right? She's beautiful and smart and kind. She's perfect."

Aspen rolled her eyes. "Still sounds like my sister. Dark hair, green eyes, able to get whatever she wants from a handsome face?"

Val squirmed. "Was you sister on an airplane tonight?"

"Yeah, she was coming home to help search for my brother."

It *was* Hazel's sister. That might make this all easier. Or harder, depending on how Aspen took the news.

"She talked about how much you loved dragons."

"She hates them." Aspen sat back in her chair with her arms crossed.

"I know. That's going to be a problem. But seeing as how her name is on my ankle, we'll make it work." Val didn't see the problem. As soon as he realized she'd sealed herself to him, he knew this was a done deal. He'd found his queen.

Runa jumped off the table. "I get to meet Aspen's sister? I must go change and make myself presentable."

Runa flew off, and Aspen frowned. "Does she know what you are?"

Val shook his head. Sid squeezed his eyes shut for a second, but he still didn't say anything.

Aspen then turned to Sid. "This is unbelievable. What are the chances that he sealed himself to my sister?"

"About as likely as you sealing yourself to me the day we met."

"But Hazel detests dragons."

"Val wasn't a dragon."

Aspen turned back to Val. "This still doesn't make sense. What about the marking? Did you two talk about that at all?"

"No. It happened just as our plane was landing. I didn't get a chance to discuss it. I figured I'd find her tomorrow." He didn't understand why they weren't more excited about this. One less thing they had worry about.

"I don't think you really know my sister. She's not into commitment. At all. She and I made a pact the summer we both got hurt that we'd never let it happen again. As far as I know, she still hasn't changed her mind."

"Yeah, she told me about that."

"She told you about that?" Aspen sat up straighter.

"She told me how she got her heart broken by Teddy and doesn't want to have anything to do with relationships."

Aspen leaned back in her chair and frowned. Obsidian rubbed the back of her neck. "But you changed your mind. Maybe she did too."

Aspen rolled her eyes. "On an airplane? Come on. Plus, she really hates dragons. I'm not sure how that happened, but something went wrong."

Val rubbed his eyes. Hazel had told him that she wasn't looking for a relationship, but Aspen made it seem like there was no way she'd love him. But that wasn't possible. Her name was on his ankle. That meant she sealed herself to him as well. Because if she hadn't, her name wouldn't have appeared. It would just be a swirl of loops.

Aspen looked at her phone. "Dammit. It's too late to go home. They won't let me in. Sissy's gonna freak when she's sees that tattoo."

"What do you mean that they won't let you in?" Val asked.

"The military. They have barricades around the park, and they close at nine p.m. No one is allowed out or in. Stupid murderous dragon." She typed quickly on her phone.

"What's she talking about?" Val asked.

Obsidian jerked his head. "Hmm. Oh, the dragon that's eating people. They shut down the park. They think he got her brother."

Aspen slammed her phone down. "It didn't get Rowan. He's alive. I know it. We just need to find him."

"How do you know he's alive?"

"He's my twin. I'd know if he were dead." Her bright green eyes now burned with determination.

She looked down at her phone.

"Sissy said she'll meet me at the Purple Dragon at eight. She'll need some explanation of the tattoo. Does she know your full name?"

"Yeah. She called it romantic." Val wanted to go with her. He desperately needed to see Hazel again.

Aspen tapped her foot. "She was probably being sarcastic. I'll need to leave out the fact that you are a dragon and that the tattoo means she'll never love anyone else. That will just scare her off."

"How are you going to explain the tattoo without explaining that I'm a dragon?" Val wished he had some grand plan on how to win her over, but he had no clue what he was doing.

"I don't know, but we'll sleep on it. Maybe I can just play dumb. Say I don't know anything more about it than she does. I'll show her mine, and we can just be dumbfounded together."

"Do you really think she'll buy it?" He frowned. Hazel was smarter than that. Plus, she wasn't the type to just accept pat answers.

"Maybe. It's that or have her run for the hills when she finds out you're a dragon."

"How are we going to get her to like dragons?" Val figured that would be their biggest obstacle. Her commitment issues wouldn't matter. Not after she sealed herself to him.

"I don't know. But leave that to me. You focus on convincing her to like you."

Val nodded. It would make everything easier if he wasn't trying to make her like dragons. He really didn't think getting her to like him would be a problem. He'd never heard of anyone who sealed to someone they didn't love or want to spend the rest of their life with. When dragons sealed together, they were already madly in love.

Sid stood. "We should get some sleep. Come on, I'll show you to your room."

"Wait, there is something else you should know."

Sid sat back down. "What's up?"

"I was attacked on the airplane. It's possible it was just a fluke, but the man who attacked me seemed pretty determined to get to me specifically."

"What do you mean?" asked Sid.

Val explained what happened on the airplane.

Sid leaned back and crossed his arms, staring off into space. Aspen's eyes flicked between him and Val, who tapped his fingers on the table. The assassination attempt bothered him.

"It does seem that his purpose was to assassinate you. I'll put out feelers and see who knows about you. I expect it has to do with the prophecy, which we'll talk about later. For now you're safe with us. Let's go to bed and worry about queens, wars, and death in the morning." Sid grinned and pulled Aspen up with him. "The love side of this is so much more fun than the wars. Don't you think?"

"Of course," Aspen replied. "Too bad, we have to go outside and, you know, actually live life."

Val followed them upstairs. He liked Sid's laid back and friendly attitude. Theo was more uptight, so he'd expected Sid to be as well. Val could see why people would follow him. He was the type of leader that won you over with his easy ways, not the type that demanded it. Val knew he would have to step up and be a king as well, and he hoped he could do it like this.

If no one else tried to kill him.

CHAPTER 8

HAZEL WOKE EARLY the next morning, if you could call what she did over the night as sleep. She barely caught a minute of shuteye, and the evidence was everywhere. Her pillows were missing from her bed, and her blankets fell off to one side.

Her room was just as she left it a year and a half ago, with the picture of the raging ocean hanging over her dresser to her forgotten surfboard behind the closet door.

Last summer her family came to visit her instead of her coming home. She had hoped to spend the time with her sister, but Aspen had disappeared into the mountains to photograph those wretched dragons. Rowan wouldn't leave the hotel room, so it was mostly just Hazel and her parents down at the beach.

She missed Aspen. A lot. They were super close before she moved away. If it hadn't been for Paul and his clinginess, she'd still be here. Maybe she shouldn't have let him run her off.

She threw on jeans and an old Gardiner High hoodie, and grinned. She hadn't worn jeans since she left home. The cold was going to kill her. Maybe it had killed Rowan. He always hated the snow and the cold. They lived in Florida when they were kids, and so he'd never built snowmen or gone sledding. Hazel remembered the first snowfall after they moved to Montana. She and Aspen had gone outside and made a massive snowman while Rowan watched from the window. His only contribution had been a broken pair of his old glasses. Now he was out in the freezing cold, possibly dead. Her stomach clenched. No, she wouldn't think of that. He was alive somewhere. He had to be.

She dug around a drawer and found some socks. When she sat down to put them on, she studied the marking on her ankle again. It didn't make sense. How did something like that just show up?

It didn't. That was the problem. Things like this didn't just happen. When did it show up? It wasn't before she got on the plane.

It was that kiss. Her ankle had burned, but she was too caught up in the moment to really give it much thought. Yeah, Val was an amazing kisser. She closed her eyes, and his face appeared in her head. She could almost smell the sea. She opened her eyes and stood up. She couldn't do this.

She wouldn't be able to avoid him because Gardiner was too small for that. She hoped he'd honor her wishes. Because seeing him again would be difficult. She couldn't kiss him. Ever. Then she might fall harder than she already had.

As she put her hand on the rail to head downstairs, she heard the sound of utensils against plates and smelled coffee brewing. Her eyebrow rose when she found her parents leaning over the table.

Mom looked up. "Hey, how'd you sleep?"

Hazel yawned and grabbed a coffee cup out of the cupboard. "Not well."

Her mom patted her hand. "None of us have."

"What's this?" Hazel asked.

"Areas we've searched and areas that still need to be scoured."

Hazel studied the map that was covered with red Xes. "It looks like most of the park has already been searched."

"We expect the initial search will be over in a few days."

"Then what?"

Her father frowned. "Then we start over, focus on hot spots, areas where he could live even in these freezing temperatures."

"This doesn't make sense though. Rowan never goes outside."

"You haven't seen him recently. He's been going out."

"Yeah, you don't go from someone who's scared to set foot in the great outdoors to someone who will take a hike in the middle of a snowstorm. None of this adds up. Is it okay if I explore some of the other possibilities? I'm not going to be much good out in the woods."

"You can focus on the town. Maybe he met a girl and refused to leave her house." Dad grinned, but Hazel's stomach twisted. This was no time for jokes.

"I'm meeting Aspen in town at eight. Can I borrow one of the cars?"

"Sure. I was going to go with your dad. Why don't you two meet us at the Tower-Roosevelt Visitor Center at ten. That will give you a couple of hours to brainstorm."

Hazel nodded and headed for the door. The cold air hit her, and she hurried to the car. She wished her parents would clean out the garage so they could park the cars in there, but it was full of years of accumulated junk.

It wasn't much warmer in the car. She pulled onto the main road. She'd never seen the park so deserted. Sure, it was winter, but there were still groups of people who came. Snow covered the pines and sparkled in the sunlight. When she drove through a valley, she saw steam rising from the vents. The air smelled of sulfur. She hoped against hope that Rowan had found a spot near one of those and kept warm.

She pulled into the parking lot of the Purple Dragon, her old stomping grounds. She'd never worked there with Aspen, but this was the place where everyone hung out.

Hazel stood on her tiptoes looking over the milling coffee drinkers. She spotted Aspen sitting at a table across the room. She waved, and Aspen wove her way through the crowded room and hugged her.

"Sissy. I missed you." They held each other a second longer than they would normally. The absence of their other sibling hung heavy in the midst.

"Me too. Though I wish I was here under better circumstances."

Aspen squeezed her hand. "I know. Are you jetlagged? Do you want to sit?"

"I'm okay. I want to get a coffee first. Mom's was no good this morning."

"I'd like to say that's because of Rowan, but you know Mom's coffee has never been good."

They waited in line, and Hazel grinned at the girl across the counter. Ella reached across and gave her a hug.

"Bout time you came home."

Ella's hair was now bright pink and clashed horribly with her Orange Crush t-shirt. "I know. How are you?"

"Good. What can I get you?"

"Vanilla latte."

"You never change, do you?"

Hazel shrugged and smiled.

Ella handed her the latte, and Hazel squeezed between tables to Aspen's favorite spot near the back of the shop. She sipped at her sweet drink and watched her sister for a second. Aspen had dark lines under her eyes, and her normally slick blonde hair was pulled back into a messy bun. Usually she kept it in braids. Aspen's eyes flicked around the shop.

"Looking for someone?" Hazel asked.

Aspen met her eyes. "Just Rowan. I look for him everywhere I go."

"We'll find him." Hazel's stomach clenched, and she took a couple of deep breaths.

"I hope so. I think Mom and Dad are losing hope. But he can't be dead."

Aspen gripped her mug, and Hazel reached over and put her hands over Aspen's.

"He's not. We have to believe that."

"Sis, it doesn't look good. And I think it's my fault he's missing." Aspen's shoulders fell, and she wouldn't meet Hazel's eyes.

Hazel leaned back and took another drink and savored the slight burn. "What makes you think that?"

"Rowan and I had been spending a lot of time together. We always hung out at Sid's house. In fact, when the dragon started eating people regularly, Mom threatened to send us to live with you, and we moved in with Sid instead. His brother and ex-girlfriend live with him."

Hazel tried to wrap her head around the whole thing. It sounded like a bad episode of *Jersey Shore*. Too many people living in one house that shouldn't be. Hazel pursed her lips. "That sounds complex."

Aspen snorted. "You have no idea. Anyway, Sid's ex, Skye, and Rowan became pretty close. The night he disappeared Sid had a family emergency. We all went to help out and forgot Rowan was sleeping in the other room. When he woke up, he would've found the house empty. He was probably out looking for us."

"Why didn't he just call?" Hazel asked.

"Yeah, he might have. But I lost my phone. I had to get a new one two days ago. Sid didn't have any missed calls though. We were out of range for most of the night."

Hazel pinched the bridge of her nose and thought. This didn't make sense. "What on earth were you doing?"

"Can't tell you that, sorry. Sid's family is pretty secretive and complicated. I'm part of it, or I wouldn't know."

"You can't just say things like that and not tell me what's going on? Is his family involved in Rowan's disappearance?"

"Oh no. Of course not. But I really can't tell you. They're very wealthy and like to keep a fairly low profile. There are things you can't know yet, but I'm not doing anything illegal." Aspen met Hazel's eyes, so she knew Aspen was telling the truth. She couldn't wrap her head around yet another mystery. Whatever they were involved with sounded complex.

"You said Rowan was close with Skye. Do you think she knows where he went?" Aspen said Sid's family wasn't part of why Rowan went missing, but Hazel wasn't convinced.

Aspen shrugged. "We can't find Skye either."

Hazel sat up straighter. How could Aspen say that without realizing the implications? "Hello, that means they're probably together."

Aspen laughed. "No, it doesn't. Skye was planning on going to see her parents. No one can get in touch with her, but it's not that unusual with Sid's family's circle. They've got people out looking for Skye to see if she knows anything. But that's highly unlikely. She was with us the night Rowan went missing."

Hazel wasn't buying it. She knew her brother, and in spite of everyone saying he was doing better, she knew people didn't change overnight. If Skye was missing, then Rowan was probably with her. Hazel opened her mouth to ask another question just as Aspen waved to someone behind her.

A young man with blonde dreads pulled a chair over from another table, flipped it around, and sat down, resting his arms on the back of the chair.

He held his hand out before his eyes met hers. "I'm Theo. Nice to finally meet Aspen's elusive sister."

Hazel's mouth had dropped open. She never thought she'd see that face again. It was not a face she wanted to see.

"Teddy," she whispered. Butterflies erupted in her stomach, and she had no idea how to react. Her breath came in rapid bursts, and she focused on slowing them to drive away the panic attack. They didn't happen very often, but that face could definitely trigger one.

His smile slipped when his face registered recognition. "Hazel, I never thought I'd see you again."

She didn't know what to say. But Teddy moved before she could think. He reached for Hazel, and without warning, his lips were on hers, driving the beginnings of her panic attack away. It was like she was on the airplane again, and when she closed her eyes, she saw Val's face. She returned the kiss eagerly, but then anger built in her chest. This was not Val. This bastard broke her heart. She pulled away and slapped him across the face. Her hand stung, but she very nearly raised it to do it again. She wanted him to feel the pain he put her through.

People around them froze and stared. Teddy held his hand to his face, his eyes revealing hurt. She didn't care. He'd hurt her worse. She stuck her face in his.

"Where have you been? Why did you leave? You think it's okay to leave a girl the way you left me? Never mind. You're despicable. I never want to see your face again."

Hazel backed away. She was surprised by her emotional reaction to him. It had been three and a half years since she'd seen him, and she thought she'd pretty much gotten over him. Sure, she'd imagined plenty what she'd like to do to him if she saw him again. Running him over with her car was one. But she was happy with her life now, so why did she care?

A couple of chairs fell behind her, and Hazel turned to look. Ella headed straight for Teddy, murder in her eyes. Without warning she punched him right in the nose.

Teddy's head snapped back and blood burst from his nose. Aspen was up out of her seat and pulled Ella away.

"Get the hell out of my shop," Ella yelled at Teddy as Aspen struggled with her.

Hazel handed Teddy a couple of napkins. She almost laughed at the absurdity.

"I take it you and Ella are dating."

He pushed the napkins to his nose. "Not anymore, I'm guessing. Sorry. It's just that I think about you all the time. I couldn't help myself."

"Right. That's why you left me." Hazel laughed derisively. He was pathetic. Seriously, what had she seen in him? At least she knew she didn't have any feelings for him anymore. Hell, when he was kissing her, she thought he was Val.

Teddy shook his head. "That was a long time ago."

Before he could say anything else, Aspen came back and handed him more napkins. "You really should go."

Teddy had his head still tilted back, and his voice came out sounding clouded. "Sid said he's going to drop Val off and come back to get you. You need to be ready in a half hour. He wants to do the southern part of the park again."

Val? Why was he talking about Val? Could this get any weirder?

Aspen put her hand on Teddy's bicep. "Go take care of your nose. I'll see you later."

He walked away, and Aspen collapsed in her chair.

"Never a dull moment. So that's Teddy?"

Hazel nodded, still in shock. Her emotions couldn't take any more. Between Rowan missing, Val and her feelings for him, and Teddy showing up out of nowhere, she didn't know how to handle all of it. In Hawaii, she'd safely tucked her emotions away and focused on fun.

"How do you know Teddy?" Hazel, asked needing answers to this. Was Teddy connected to Val? That would be too much.

"He's Sid's brother."

Hazel rolled her eyes. "Also did he say something about Val?"

Aspen nodded. "Yep. Val's Sid's cousin. Told me he met you on the airplane."

Hazel put her head in her hands and tried to think.

"So you're telling me that Teddy is Sid's brother and Val is Sid's cousin? This is messed up."

Aspen took a sip of her mocha and gave Hazel a grin. "No kidding. Val wants to see you again though. Do you want to do dinner with us tonight?"

Hazel focused on the problem at hand. "We need to find Rowan, not worry about my love life. Besides, things with Val were too real. I don't want to see him again."

"I thought you'd say that. He's a nice guy though. He'd be good for you."

Hazel shrugged. "Maybe, but I can't worry about that now. Will you help me search around town? See if we can find stuff Mom and Dad missed?"

Aspen shook her head. "Nope, I go with Sid. We cover more ground that way. Do things outside of the scope of the government's search."

"You can't go out alone. That's dangerous."

Aspen leaned forward, her eyes narrowed. "Everything about this is dangerous. I'm actually safer than most people. But I can't take you with me. Sid and Theo are usually with me. I expect Val will join us as well."

"Why can't I come with?"

"Because we cover massive amounts of ground." Aspen looked away from her. "I can't tell you how. It's a secret."

"We don't have secrets."

Aspen snorted. "Yeah, we do, Sis. I can't tell you about this, but trust me. I can cover more ground without you. You'll be better off searching with Mom and Dad."

"You're not making sense." Hazel creased her eyebrows.

"I expect a lot of things don't make sense. Like why Rowan was out in the woods anyway. Like Teddy being here. Like that marking on your ankle."

Hazel gasped. "How do you know about that?"

"Because I have one too. Come over tonight, and we'll explain some things. Well, I can explain everything except the mark. No one knows why they are showing up. But I can help you understand the rest. For now though, we need to focus on Rowan. I have to go."

No flipping way. Aspen had one too? Hazel felt a sense of relief. At least she wasn't crazy. Aspen stood, and Hazel grabbed her arm. "You can't just leave. You need to explain."

Aspen shook her head. "Sorry, I need to go find Rowan. Come to dinner. Seriously. The boys can answer questions that I can't. Gotta run. Love you, Sis. See you tonight."

Aspen stood and slipped between the tables before Hazel could argue. But Hazel wasn't letting her get away. As she was about to stand up, another person sat in the seat Aspen just vacated. It was the third to last person she wanted to see.

Paul.

CHAPTER 9

"**W**HEN DID YOUR gorgeous self arrive?" Paul asked.

"Last night." Hazel wasn't sure she could handle any more drama. Though with the exception of the time he proposed out of nowhere, he was usually pretty drama free. That was what she liked best about him.

He looked good and had filled out since she left. A five o'clock shadow made him look sexy along with the army fatigues he wore. They had a complicated history, but they started out as best friends in middle school. Then when she came back from Yosemite with her heart broken, he had been her shoulder to cry on. Eventually they moved into the murky area where they made out but put no labels on it. She dated other people, and he seemed okay with it, but he'd thrown her for a loop when he proposed.

She ran. They still kept up a little via Facebook, but she kept him at arm's length.

"I don't remember you mentioning you were military," Hazel said.

"National Guard. We got called up to deal with the Yellowstone issue. But it's spread now." He ran a hand through his shaggy blonde hair, and it fell into his eyes. Hazel put her hands in her lap so she wasn't tempted to brush it out. She had enough boy drama with Teddy and Val. She didn't need to add Paul to mix.

"What do you mean?" she asked, genuinely curious. She hoped he wouldn't mistake it for interest in him.

"You haven't heard? There was a death in Hawaii at Volcanoes National Park."

"What?"

Rowan needed to remain the center of their search. Not some other poor soul in a different park. She knew that was selfish of her to think that, but if deaths were happening in other parts of the country, the government might shift resources, and right now, she wanted everyone looking for Rowan.

"No witnesses, but it left behind a hand, just like the early deaths here."

"Damned dragons. What do you think will happen?"

Paul shrugged. "Dunno, but the fact it's happening that far away isn't a good thing. It means there's more than one."

"Either that or this one has moved. Maybe it couldn't take the heat here in Yellowstone. Too many people looking for it." Hazel took a drink of her latte that had now gone cold.

"Maybe, but it will have a harder time hiding in Hawaii. Think about it. The dragons here are all silver and gold. Down there they're all bright red."

Hazel bit her lip. She couldn't keep all that was happening straight. She took a deep breath and remembered the only thing that mattered.

"Have you heard anything about my brother?"

Paul's face softened. "I've been helping with the search. Your parents are holding up really well. I was surprised. They've been super focused on the search and patient with those in charge."

Hazel nodded. "My parents have always been like that."

"Do you remember that time we brought Rowan with us to the movies?" Paul gave her a grin she always loved and scooted closer to her.

Hazel laughed. "Yeah, and he accidentally spilled his Coke all over the man sitting in front of him when the dinosaur ate the crazy girl."

"Then we had to run out of there so the guy didn't beat the shit out of him."

Hazel felt the tears starting before she could stop them. "What if we don't find him?" she asked with a cracking voice.

Paul slid over to her and pulled her into his arms. "Hey, don't think like that. He's alive. We'll find him. Come on, I'll help you. Where do you want to start looking?"

Hazel pulled out of his embrace. "How are you going to do that? You've got to work."

"What do you think my work is these days?"

Being with Paul was nice and comfortable. Plus he understood how important it was to her to find her brother. He'd help her.

She sniffed. "Thanks, that means a lot to me."

He lifted her chin so she was looking right at him. "Haz, I'd do anything for you. You know that."

She nodded with a sinking stomach. She'd hoped he'd go back to just being her friend, but the look in his eyes was one of desire, not friendship. She'd use him though, if she had to. Her brother was the most important thing, and if Paul's feelings were a casualty, she wouldn't hesitate to sacrifice them.

CHAPTER 10

VAL RAN A razor along his chin. Getting ready as a human was a hell of a lot harder than as a dragon. He'd seen humans grooming when he watched them camping, but he never realized how much work it was. His hand shook a little, and he took a deep breath. He was trying not to think about what today would bring.

He would see his dad, learn more about what his duties would be as king, and if he was lucky, see Hazel again. The last one made him the most nervous. Aspen acted like Hazel wouldn't give him the time of day.

He washed off his face and made his way down the stairs to the kitchen. He looked at the pictures on the wall as he walked. He supposed the artwork was pretty, but it didn't capture the true beauty of things. He preferred seeing the actual landscapes and people to just an image of them.

"Good morning," Sid said, grabbing a carton of milk out of the fridge. "Grab three bowls, will you?" He pointed to the cupboard behind Val's head. Val turned around and opened the door. "Also, get a couple of spoons from the drawer next to you."

Val took his wares to the table. Sid brought the milk and cereal.

"Who's the third bowl for?" Val asked.

"Me." Runa appeared at his shoulder. "Captain Crunch is my favorite. Lucky Charms is good too, but Raisin Bran is gross."

"Don't listen to her. Raisin Bran is the best," Sid replied.

Runa landed on the table. "Well, we can't all be perfect, Your Highness." Runa nudged at a red box on the table. "Try the Captain Crunch."

Val sat down. "Okay. I'll try it."

"Get me a bowl too," Runa chirped.

"Of course." He poured out the cereal and milk into the two bowls. He picked up his spoon, but Runa dunked her head and slurped noisily.

Sid shook his head. "No manners, that one."

Runa's head popped up. "You try eating this with no hands. I dare you."

"No, thanks. There are few advantages to being human. This is one of them." He held up his spoon.

"What's on the agenda for today?" Val asked.

"When we're done eating, I'm going to take you to see your father. I promised him he could see you right away."

"Do you know him well?"

"I do. But I didn't know about you until last year. Your father is a complex dragon and pretty secretive. I was surprised as hell when he finally told me why he was banished."

"Do you think he'll tell me?"

"Of course. Believe it or not, you'd be here right now even if you weren't king. This actually makes it more complicated because I can't just let you stay with him for longer than a few hours. After I take you to him, I need to go help Aspen search for Rowan. Then tonight, we need to start preparing for the war."

Val ran his hand through his hair. "I still don't quite get the war thing. I mean Theo told me turning black was a fulfillment of the three kings prophecy, but to be honest, I don't even know what the prophecy says. Sure I've heard the story, but it's been told in several different ways by different people."

Sid sighed. "Yeah, that's part of the problem. We are trying to locate the original source of the prophecy, but so far we haven't had much luck. The original is written down in Everett's cave. Before he died he gave me what he remembered."

"Did he tell you where to find his cave?" Val had heard of the old dragon that had been around since the dragon wars. He didn't know Everett had passed on.

"No. He died before he got the chance. I have dragons searching for his cave though. It's got to be here in Yellowstone somewhere."

"So exactly what does the prophecy say?" This was important. It held his fate.

"Three kings will rise from the land, the sea, and fire. Together they will battle the snow witch. The war will be one the world never forgets. Species against species. Brother against brother. Who will win, no one knows. If it be the witch, she will enslave all of humanity. If it be the kings, only one survives."

Val rubbed his hand across his face and sighed. "I've never heard that version."

"Yeah, I know. It wasn't quite how I remembered it either."

"Does it mean that all species will fight in the war, including humans?"

"Maybe. It's hard to say. I really need to read it for myself. I'm most concerned that only one of us will survive. Also, there's no telling how long this war will last. It could be centuries. We need to prepare for that possibility. We don't know when the war will actually start."

"Do we know who the snow witch is?"

"No. The only one who made sense died."

"Do you have any training, any ideas on how to handle this? I know you are new to the throne."

"Ha! I wish. No. I'm going to consult with a few of the older dragons. Your father, for one. We have warriors trained in the royal dragons, but none of them have seen war. Until we know what we are up against, I can't make a plan of attack. But even as we speak, I've got ambassadors making nice with all the dragon races. Your presence still isn't known, so most don't know that the prophecy is being fulfilled. Once it becomes public, dragons will start taking sides."

Val would have to process all of this eventually, but right now his mind was stuck on one thought. "Why would you consult with my father?"

Sid gave him a small smile. "Because your father knows how to fight."

Runa poked her head up. "Aspen is back." She took off from the table, and Val heard a crash. Aspen yelled out.

"Watch where you're going." She walked into the kitchen rubbing her chest. "She flew right into me."

Theo followed, carrying a dazed looking Runa. Aspen gave Val a cheeky grin.

"You got under her skin."

"What do you mean?"

"She said she doesn't want to see you again."

Val's chest tightened. That wasn't the reaction he was looking for. "Why?"

"Because it was 'too real.' Her words, not mine. But I think I dangled enough mystery under her nose that she'll come to dinner. Theo really shouldn't be here. Or should I call you Teddy?" She looked at Theo with her eyes dancing.

Theo rubbed at his red nose. "She was the only one who every called me that."

"Wait, you're Teddy?" Val asked. His thoughts raced, trying to put Theo together with Teddy.

Theo nodded.

"You crushed her." Val stood, his chair crashing to floor behind him, rage building in his chest. This was the man who broke her heart. Theo held up his hands.

"Please don't hit me. I'm a little over that by now."

Val looked down, both confused by his anger and his desire to hit Theo. Because in spite of Theo asking him not to hit him, Val was seriously considering it.

Aspen giggled. "Hazel slapped him, and then Ella punched him in the nose. Go ahead Val punch him in the gut."

Theo moved around the table and sat down. "You know why I had to leave her, right?"

Aspen shook her head. Val sank into his chair again, his rage simmering just underneath his skin, but he wanted to hear this story probably as much Aspen did.

"Because I almost sealed myself to her. She was the most beautiful thing I'd ever seen. I left before I did anything stupid. I'm sure she was hurt, but I had no other choice."

Aspen crossed her arms and glared at him. "Well, because of you, she won't commit to anyone. She usually dates two or three people at once to avoid getting too attached. You should probably leave town. We want to make it easy for Val to win her over."

Val listened intently. He wanted Theo to leave, but he also wanted to know how to win over Hazel. Theo did it once, so maybe he could tell him what he knew.

Sid leaned forward. "We need someone to go spy on the arctic dragons. You're good friends with Candide. Maybe you could spend a few weeks up there and see what's going on."

Theo shrugged and fingered his dreads. "Whatever will help us. Sure. My human skin is getting old anyway. It will be nice to just be a dragon for a while."

"Send regular reports via the eagles. Even if the intel seems insignificant, it could be important."

Theo stood and gave a little bow. "Of course, I still need to finish a job around here, but I'll leave in a couple of days. Good luck, Val."

Val nodded to him. Sid's eyes followed Theo as he left the room.

Aspen laid her hand over his. "You okay?"

Sid sighed. "He's acting weird."

Aspen frowned. "I think it's still because he's not used to you being king. We don't have time to worry about that though. We need to search for Rowan."

"We should drop Val off first. You ready to go see your dad?" Sid asked.

He'd been looking forward to meeting his dad for a long time, but he was nervous. No one told him why his dad was banished, and he was scared to find out. What if he didn't like his father? The dragons that raised him were good, warm, and friendly. But he knew he didn't really belong. They made sure he always had enough to eat and trained him in the ways of the fire dragons, but he always felt like he was missing out on something. He supposed that was why he spent so much time watching the humans. Now he was about to meet his real father.

Sid nudged him. "Let's go. We'll need to change."

They exited out of the back door and into the middle of the yard. Aspen stood a little ways from them, shivering in spite of a thick coat and hat. They changed into their dragon forms, and Aspen gasped.

"Two black dragons. Amazing," she said and laid her hand on both of their flanks.

We just need to find the third, Sid said.

Any ideas where he might be? Val was curious about who this third dragon could be. He wouldn't feel so confused and alone in this with a brother to share it with.

No. I've got eagles and a handful of royal dragons all over the nation searching for him. It makes it harder that we can't reveal what we're looking for, but I think the secrecy is important. Though I'm sure rumors have already started. He could be anywhere. Obviously, we think he's a sea dragon, but they are hard to find since they spend so much time under the water.

Val hoped they found him soon. The war seemed pressing, and the sooner all three of them were together, the sooner they could create a plan of attack for the unknown snow witch, rather than just reacting to the things happening around them, like the human killings and attempt on his life.

Bright circles on Sid's chest drew Val's eyes.

Are those loyalty seals? I've never seen them before.

Yes. Aspen and I were not supposed to be together. I was trying to prevent being killed. I've got all but a canyon dragon. I would complete it, but with the war pending, I need all the support I can get, and I don't want to give the current council a reason to turn against me.

But wouldn't that stop a war? Don't the loyalty symbols make you invincible?

Not exactly. It prevents another council from forming, but I think the arctic dragons have something else in mind.

Aspen scrambled up on Sid's back as Val studied the marks.

My father's name is on your chest.

Yes. He was one of the first. Very loyal. He'll be an asset in the war.

Val didn't like thinking about the war. He wasn't a trained fighter. Not to mention there was a good chance he would die before it was all over.

Sid took off, and Val followed. The air here was much colder than he was used to, but he didn't mind. White covered the ground below, except where steam rose from deep blue pools.

After we drop you off, we're going to search for Aspen's brother. Do you think you can find your way back to the house?

Val turned to Obsidian. *Of course. Good luck in the search. I'll help when I'm finished.*

We'll come home for lunch. You can come out with us after that.

They flew in between two mountains and into a cave. They landed in a cavern, in front of a deep red dragon. Val took a step back when Damien stepped into the light. His father's jaw was wrong, and he had no tail. Val wondered if there were unseen injuries as well.

Val, meet Damien. Your father. Then Obsidian flew out of the cave.

This was his father. Damien didn't say anything as Val circled him. He had a sealing on his ankle with the name Hestia. It was a dark maroon but slightly faded. It looked similar to the one on Val's ankle, but the words around Hestia's name were different.

Was Hestia my mother? Val finally asked. His feelings were all mixed up. He wanted to hear more about this dragon who gave him life, but part of him was still a little bitter that he was left to be raised by others.

Yes. I loved her very much.

What happened to her?

She got sick and died.

Did she suffer? How long was she sick?

For a few years. You were a very young dragon. I don't expect you to remember it. The elders took you from me shortly after that.

Val wanted to ask why his father let him go, but he felt a slow anger building in his chest. He'd been abandoned. His father had just given him up to the elders and disappeared. What kind of a father did that?

I'm very glad you are here. I haven't seen you since you were a baby. I've missed you. Thank you for coming. Damien shifted nervously and studied Val. Val tried to be sympathetic, but he couldn't.

Why? He snarled. This was his father, and he hadn't bothered to even try to contact him in over five hundred years.

Why what?

Why haven't you seen me since I was a baby? Val raised his head high so that he looked down on his father.

Damien shuffled back a few steps. *The elders banned me from the islands. They said if I returned, they would kill me. What use would I be to you dead?*

You weren't much use to me anyway. Val knew he was being mean, but he couldn't help it. He'd envisioned this moment so many times since he found out Damien was alive, and he couldn't fathom a father that wouldn't even try to let him know he was alive. He could've sent a royal dragon or an eagle. But he just let Val believe he was dead.

Damien raised his head, meeting Val's eyes. *I had no choice. You can hold that against me, or you can accept that I'm willing to help you now. Who do you think is going to teach you to fight, son? You've got a war coming, and I'll see to it that you know how to not only defend yourself, but win.*

Val wondered briefly what on earth got him banned from the islands in the first place. How he could do something that would make them relinquish his son? Val snorted and was startled by the black smoke instead of red. For a moment he'd forgotten his scales had changed color.

Forgive me for being rude, but based on your injuries, I'd say you don't know much about fighting.

Damien moved forward. *You see these gashes across my chest?*

Val wasn't sure where his father was going with this.

The woodland dragons have offered to heal them numerous times, but I always decline. Do you want to know why?

Maybe he was about to get some of the answers he wanted. Val relaxed his shoulders. *Why?*

Because they are from you. You clung to me when they ripped you away. I won't let them be healed because I wanted the reminder of you.

Val's heart stilled. He didn't know how to respond. He had assumed that his father had gotten in a fight that went wrong. This was news to him. The fact that his father fought to keep him. *Now that I'm here, will you let them heal you?*

Damien sighed. *Maybe.*

Val hesitated again, still a little nervous about asking the question. *Why did they take me from you?*

I'm not proud of this story. Know that. I made a lot of mistakes, but this was the biggest one. I wasn't in control of my emotions. It's not an excuse, but I was grieving deeply. Your mother died, and I was so angry. I lashed out at the woodland dragons who had tried to heal her and killed one of them. It wasn't an accident, but it wasn't on purpose either. My own emotions blinded me. I could see nothing, only my rage. When I returned to the islands with you, the elders took you from me and banished me.

The royal dragons gave me a home. Obsidian's mother had a lot to do with that. I've been here ever since. I can't fly long distances, though I thought about coming to find you several times. I'm glad you are here now.

This was definitely not the story Val had expected. He moved a few steps toward his father and nudged his head against his father's jaw. *Thank you for sharing that with me. I don't know quite what to say.*

You don't have to say anything. Are you willing to give me a chance?

Of course. He wanted to say something else. Something that he'd dreamed of saying for years but never had the privilege. He forged on. *Dad.* Val jerked his head up. *But you have to do one thing for me.*

What's that?

Get those gashes healed. You might want to let them take care of your wings and jaw as well.

Damien thought for a second. *Okay, I'll have Athena fetch Jolantha.*

Who's Athena?

Obsidian's mother. She and I were good friends when we were young. Her mate has passed away recently, and I've been helping her cope. She's still pretty angry, but she's starting to soften.

Val spent the next few hours talking with his father. He'd never felt so comfortable in his life. This was very different than it had been with his aunt and uncle.

I know you have to go soon, but would you like a short lesson first? Damien asked.

Sure.

Okay, what do you think is the most vulnerable part of a dragon's body? Val thought for a second. *The neck?*

Damien snorted poofs of red smoke. *That's what most people think, so your first tip is to protect your neck. Most dragons will attack there first. If you have a clear opening, definitely try, but if you want to surprise a dragon, go for his eyes. If you can blind him, you'll have the advantage.*

What if someone else does it to me first? How do I fight if I'm blind?

That takes instinct and time. We'll practice that. If you practice blind, you'll learn how to fight blind.

Val knew it was time for him to go, but he wasn't ready to leave his father. He'd just found him again. *I have to go help Obsidian and Aspen search for her brother. Would you like to come?*

I'm going to take care of these injuries, but maybe tomorrow.

Thanks, Dad, for all your help. I know I have a lot of responsibilities now, but I'll come see you whenever I can.

I'd like that. Now get out of here. I wouldn't want to you to get in trouble with Aspen.

You mean Obsidian?

No, I mean Aspen. She's the fierce one.

Val took one more look at his father and then spread his wings and flew out of the cave. Val flew south, toward Sid's house. On the way he thought about his father. It'd been five hundred years. How would Damien make up all that time? He was quiet and soft spoken, and he seemed to genuinely want to know him. Val liked him. But his stomach felt hollow. He would never be able to have a normal relationship with his father. Val was a king now, and a war was on the horizon. He'd have other responsibilities.

As he came over the mountain, he spotted the mansion. He caught a flutter of wings out of the corner of his eyes and a sharp pain pierced his side. Then another one stung his neck. He dropped a few feet and swung his head around to see what had hurt him. A swarm of hawks descended. They tore at his wings and bit and clawed at him. He tucked his wings and dove for Sid's house. The hawks continued to follow him, but as he crossed the tree line another swarm of birds flew toward him as well. Dread filled his chest. He didn't know if he was going to make it. But this new group of birds didn't come after him. They went straight for the hawks. A weight lifted off him as he landed on the ground in front of Sid's back door. The eagles that had protected him gathered around him seconds later, and Sid flew out of the house with Aspen at his heels.

"Are you okay?" Sid's face was ashen.

Val looked down at his body covered with tiny holes and scratches.

He took a couple of deep breaths. *I'm fine, I think. It's mostly super-ficial. Why would the hawks try to kill me?*

Sid turned to the eagles. "Did you have any of your brothers follow the hawks? We need to know why they attacked him."

Aspen circled him. "I don't see any that look deep. The gashes in your wings look awful though."

"Dammit, follow them. I've got this here," Sid yelled.

The eagles took off in a flurry of wings.

"The eagles all came with you. They didn't bother to see where the hawks came from. What happened?"

They came out of nowhere. Someone wants me dead. For the first time, Val felt real fear over what he'd gotten into. His life on the island was so quiet. The most drama he'd ever found was when a couple of humans had spotted him spying and freaked out. He'd hidden in a cave for weeks after that. Now here he was on the mainland with two attempts on his life in a matter of two days.

Sid ran a hand over his face. "This is the second time someone has tried to kill you. My guess would be it's the arctic dragons, and this means they know. We've got to find this third dragon, get you a queen, and prepare for this war."

I agree, but first, can you summon a healer? My wounds are all super-ficial, but it hurts.

"No need, I can do it." Sid clapped his hands together and walked around Val.

What? How?

Sid grinned. "Do you know why it's so important that we have strong queens?"

No.

"Because the council members give her their gifts, which we get when we are bonded. She has to be strong enough to accept the gifts. If she's not, then she could be so overwhelmed by the gifts that they would kill her. It's why the testing was created. Actually, Aspen, would you like to try first? Just on one of the scratches. I can take care of the rest."

"I don't even know what to do."

"You just need practice accessing the gift of healing. It will tell you what to do. Go ahead, pick a spot, and give it a whirl."

Aspen placed her hand over one of Val's injuries. After a minute, she squealed. "I did it. Look." Val looked down, and sure enough the scratch was gone. Would Hazel be strong enough to withstand the gifting? She was certainly strong-willed, but would that make her a good queen?

Sid gave her a quick kiss. "Good job. Now watch."

Sid transformed into a dragon and placed his snout on Val's head. Val felt warmth spread from his forehead to his tail. When Sid removed his snout, the pain was gone.

It's imperative that you win over Hazel right away. You are being targeted, and you need the extra gifts. I have a feeling this war's going to start faster than any of us are prepared for.

CHAPTER 11

"**A** HUMVEE, HUH?" Hazel stared at the monster vehicle in front of her.

Paul gave her a grin. "I wish I could say it was mine. It's the Guards'. I couldn't afford it."

Hazel climbed in. It smelled of sweat and cigars.

"Why's the National Guard all involved?" Hazel asked.

"Because this dragon is wicked dangerous."

Hazel fiddled with the glove box. "That's crazy. Does the government have a plan if he's not caught?"

"We'll get rid of them. People won't complain. Maybe then, we can actually use the national parks."

Hazel had been saying that for years. But Aspen and Val would be upset. She supposed they'd get over losing the dragons. "No complaints here. How would they do it?"

Paul shrugged as he pulled onto the road to the park.

"I'm not privy to that information, but I expect they will poison their food source or something. Nuke their nests maybe. It will take several years to get rid of them all."

Paul flashed an ID at the guard at the gate. Military vehicles were everywhere, and troops holding massive guns paced in front of the gates.

"I've never seen anything like this."

He gave her a crooked grin. "It looks like we are at war. I've never been a part of anything like this. The thing is, no one sees anything. The most they've had to do is chase out teenagers who try to sneak in to go snowmobiling."

"So you're not seeing any dragons?" Hazel tried to look out the windshield, but it was hard to see the sky.

"We see them all the time. But supposedly only one is dangerous, so we are not to engage unless we feel like the dragon is going to eat us. But I still get nervous when I see one. We've been told the dragons are searching for the killer as well. Though how they know that is beyond me. They're animals."

Hazel looked out her own window and saw several gold and silver specks circling high in the sky. One of those gold specks could be the killer. She shivered.

"Someone knows how to communicate with them then. Any ideas who?"

Paul laughed. "I'd start with your sister."

"Aspen?"

"Look, I've been on the search from nearly day one, and she's never with us. She goes out with the dragons. I've even seen her riding on a massive black one."

Hazel had a hard time believing that one. "Are you serious?"

"Yeah, but I don't think I was supposed to know that. I'm not sure your parents even know. They think she's out with her rich boyfriend searching in a helicopter."

"Did you tell anyone you'd seen her?"

"My commanding officer. He told me to keep my trap shut."

"Why are you telling me?"

Paul grabbed Hazel's hand. "Come on, you know I tell you everything. I always have. I know we haven't talked much since you moved to Hawaii, but I still trust you."

Paul pulled up in front of the visitor center and turned to her. He grabbed both of her hands and looked deep into her eyes.

"Look, I don't know what you were told. But Hazel, it's been a week. You know that right now they're just looking for a body. There is no way he's alive. Not in this weather. It's too cold. I don't think they are going to even find a body. If that dragon ate him, he didn't leave any evidence."

Hazel jerked her hands out of his, her stomach twisting. "You're wrong."

"You need to accept he's probably dead. It will make the rest of this so much easier."

She glared at him and then got out of the car. Rowan wasn't dead. He couldn't be. Her pulse sped up as she thought of the possibility. Was she the only one who still held out hope?

She stomped into the visitor center. Her parents were standing around a table with the same map from the kitchen.

Her mom turned to her, an ever present frown on her face. "Hey, how are you doing?"

"Is it true?" Hazel crossed her arms and tapped her foot, blinking back the tears. How could they think he was dead?

"Is what true?"

She leaned forward and hissed. "Are we just looking for a body?"

"No, of course not. Who told you that?" Mom laid her hand on Hazel's shoulder and looked her right in the eyes.

Hazel took a deep breath, relief flooding her. "Okay, so you think he's still alive?"

"I have to. Even if it is unlikely." Mom's eyes filled with tears, and Hazel instantly felt guilty for making her worry.

Hazel grabbed her mom's hands. "He's alive, and we're going to find him."

"Of course we will."

"Is it possible that he's not in the park? What do you know about his disappearance?"

"Not much. The last person to see him alive was Aspen. He was with her and her friends. She went out with Sid, and when she came back, he was gone. It was like he just vanished."

"Why search the park?"

"Because Aspen left her jeep at Sid's house, and they found it on the side of the road, down the street from our house. It wouldn't start. We had to take it to the shop. We think he left it there and tried to walk home."

"Who was on duty at the guard station? The park was already shut down. Someone had to let him in."

Hazel's parents looked at each other. "We never thought of that."

"Really? Who's the official detective on the case?"

"There isn't one. The park rangers and National Guard are leading the search."

"Doesn't the FBI get involved in missing person cases?"

"The FBI wouldn't get involved in a simple missing person's case. Not like this."

Hazel sighed. "Okay, can you find out who was on duty?"

Dad nodded and went back into an office. Paul put his hand on her back. Hazel pinched the bridge of her nose. "I can't believe they waited a week to tell me. If he was abducted, he could be anywhere."

Dad came back with a note. "Jeff Daniels was on duty. He's off today. I tried his cell, but he's not answering. This is his address if you want to go visit him."

"What makes you think he'll be home if he didn't answer his phone?"

Dad shuffled. "I don't know. But we should have confirmation on this, so I think you should follow up with him. Plus, it's safer for you to chase this lead than be here in the park. We don't need you freezing to death too."

"Too? So you think he's dead?" She was tired of people giving up on Rowan so quickly. He couldn't be dead.

Dad rubbed his hand across his face. "The thought's occurred to me. But I'm not giving up yet." At least he hadn't lost all hope. Hazel didn't know what she would do when that happened. No, she told herself, that wouldn't happen because they were going to find him.

"Well then, I guess I'll go check out this lead." She spun on Paul. "Can you take me?"

"Let's go."

"Aren't you on duty?" She narrowed her eyes at him.

He gave her a sheepish grin. "Yeah."

"Then why can you come with me?"

"Because I've been assigned to keep an eye on you."

Hazel's insides burned. "Why?"

"Your parents don't want to lose another child, so they asked us to assign someone to stay with you. I volunteered. I figured you'd be happy to spend time with me."

Hazel exhaled. She couldn't believe they were coddling her like that. "I don't need a babysitter."

Paul held out his keys. "I'm your ride. Do you want to talk to Mr. Daniels or not?"

Hazel hated he knew her well enough that she wouldn't waste time arguing with him when there was a lead to follow.

It took about thirty minutes to get to Mr. Daniels's house. Paul caught her up on all the gossip she missed since she'd left. She barely heard it. She couldn't believe no one bothered to question him. Or maybe they had and were just letting her go to get her out of the main investigation.

Mr. Daniels answered the door right away. He was a tired looking man with a high forehead and weak chin. Hazel didn't bother making small talk.

"My name is Hazel. My brother, Rowan, went missing last week. I was wondering if I could ask you a couple of questions."

He waved her in. "Your dad just called. Sorry I didn't answer the phone earlier. I was in the shower. Come on in."

"Thanks." She entered the tiny house and took off her hat and gloves. She left her coat on.

They sat on a tattered couch. "You were on gate duty that night. My parents found my sister's jeep on the street near our home, which means Rowan would've gone through your gate. Do you remember seeing him?"

He rubbed his chin. "I remember seeing the jeep, but I don't think Rowan was driving it. In fact, I'm not sure I saw Rowan at all. But I didn't look in the car too closely. I recognized it as Aspen's jeep, and I just let it go through."

"So you didn't see who was driving it?" Hazel leaned forward, her knees bouncing.

"It was dark. But I don't remember thinking anything unusual. I figured Aspen was driving."

"Did you actually see Aspen driving?"

"I told you that I didn't look that close. But a blonde girl driving a jeep passed through those gates all the time. What was I supposed to think?"

Hazel knees stopped bouncing. "Are you sure it was a girl?" This was something. Had Aspen been lying about where she was that night? Did she have something to do with Rowan's disappearance? Or was she just hiding what she knew?

"I dunno. Maybe. I really can't remember. I don't remember thinking anything looked unusual. But maybe. It was dark." The man looked flustered. "I don't know why you guys keep coming and asking me questions. I told Aspen I didn't know either."

"Aspen came to see you?" Hazel wasn't sure anything else would surprise her now.

"Yeah, the day after he went missing. I feel horrible about it. Especially because I wasn't really paying attention. If I had been, maybe I'd be more help. But your sister came in late all the time. Really, by then it was early morning. I was just ready for my shift to be over."

Hazel stood, not really caring much about his guilt. "Thank you, Mr. Daniels. I appreciate what you told us."

As soon as they got in the car, Hazel turned to Paul. "We need to go back to the spot where they found the car. Then I want to check out the jeep."

"Sure." He rested his arm across the back of her seat. He didn't touch her, but she knew he was moving in that direction. She had to bite her tongue. She wanted to tell him to not use this situation to try to win her back, but she didn't want to lose her ride. Plus, he was good at listening to her think out loud.

The spot the car was found was easy to find. There was police tape all around the area, though it was already starting to sag.

"Has it snowed since he went missing?" Hazel asked, realizing that would be a problem.

"Yeah, but not heavily. We can probably still see the tracks and footprints."

They found the tire tracks. Hazel searched the area around them. Footprints were everywhere.

"There's no way to tell if he walked or not. Too many people have been in and out of here," Hazel said as she studied the footprints that were slightly snow covered. This wasn't going to work. Maybe she could see the original pictures from the scene.

"How do you know this stuff?" Paul asked.

"I took a criminal justice class last semester. It was one of my favorite classes. I got an A." She had wondered if maybe she should pursue a career in forensics. Her counselor told her it was time for her make a decision about her major.

Paul laughed. "Hazel Winters, detective. It has a nice ring."

"Ha ha. I'm just glad I took the class now. Who knew I'd have to use the things I learned this fast." She wasn't an expert by any means, but she could sure try.

Paul leaned down next to her and studied the footprints on the ground. "Your parents told me there were no footprints. But I can see a few where he got out of the car, but nothing after that. He could've easily walked on the road. They plowed it that night, so there's no way to tell."

Hazel walked over to where the snow had been torn up and mixed with grass and dirt. It was right in front of the jeep tracks.

"What happened here?" Hazel asked.

Paul rubbed the back of his neck. "No one knows for sure, but there is speculation."

"And that is?"

"Dragon."

Hazel shook her head. No way. If that was the case, then he was dead. "I have a hard time believing Rowan would get out of the car in the first place. But he definitely wouldn't if a dragon had landed in front of him. He'd hide in the car."

Paul blew on his hands. "It's possible he got out of the car before the dragon landed. It's cold. You ready to go?"

Hazel nodded. "Do you know where the car is?"

"No, but your parents will. Let's go."

The sky turned gray as they drove toward the visitor center. "Is it getting dark already?" Haze asked, looking out the window into the shadowed woods.

"Yeah, the sun sets at around five-thirty. You might have to wait until tomorrow to see the car. You interested in dinner tonight?"

Hazel thought about this morning. Seeing Teddy. She needed to talk to Aspen, but she didn't particularly want to see Teddy, and she knew he'd be there. Plus, there was Val. She couldn't allow herself to see him again. She wanted answers, but her head spun with all the questions. What Aspen was up to and the deal with Val needed to wait until after she found Rowan.

"Sure. I'm supposed to meet up with Aspen, but I'd rather stay with you."

Paul was easy. There were no expectations, no commitments. Well, he might be angling for something more, but he also knew she would run if he got too close. He could take her mind off things for a few hours, and she could still focus on Rowan. Val though, she'd give him her heart without even knowing what happened.

CHAPTER 12

VAL LOOKED at the phone in Aspen's hand.

Going out to dinner with Paul. See you tomorrow. We need to talk.

"Why isn't she coming over tonight?" Val asked. "And who is this Paul?" Val clenched his jaw. Hazel should be here with him, not out with some other guy.

Runa, who had been sitting on the other side of Aspen, stuck her head up. Today it was jet black. "I'd say she's ditching you. But that's just my opinion."

"Runa!" Aspen exclaimed. "That's not nice. Apologize."

Runa brought her face only a few inches from Aspen's nose. "No. Who seals themselves to someone and then avoids them? She's not coming because she's scared of what will happen if she sees Val."

Val's stomach tightened. He knew she was speaking the truth. Hazel told him she didn't want anything serious. And if she felt any of the same things he did during that kiss, she'd know things had to be serious.

Aspen pushed Runa out of her face and frowned at Val. "I think she's right. Hazel is terrified of commitment. You probably make her feel things she doesn't want to. And it's all that one's fault." Aspen pointed to Theo.

"What'd I do?" he asked around a mouthful of ice cream.

"You ditched her in California. The week after that we spent the entire time crying on each other's shoulders. She loved you. In fact, she never had a serious relationship after that. She's spent the last few years trying to forget you."

Theo pushed his bowl aside and leaned forward. "Aspen, we've been over this. You know I couldn't stick around and risk sealing myself to her." Runa stuck her head in Theo's bowl and licked his ice cream. He jerked it away. "Get your own."

"You ate it all, you dummy. Aspen said she's not going to the store until tomorrow."

"Actually, Theo, can you go for me? I've got to deal with my sister, and we need to figure out how to expand the search for Rowan. I'm afraid they're going to declare him dead tomorrow."

"Can't," he said. "I'm heading up to Alaska first thing in the morning."

"Oh yeah, I forgot. What do you think you'll find?"

"The prophecy said that an evil queen will rise from the arctic tribe, but Winerva was the only one who made sense. Seeing as how you killed her, we don't know who it is. It's hard to fight against an unknown enemy. Me being gone will allow Val to pursue Hazel unimpeded too. Where is Sid anyway?" Theo asked.

"Visiting his mom. I stay home when he goes to see her," Aspen responded.

"Why?" Val asked.

"Because she hates me. But Sid visits her a lot since his dad died. I don't mind as long as I don't have to go with." Aspen scratched Runa under the chin.

"What happened to his dad?" Val asked.

"He was tracking the human killer and was murdered." Aspen wouldn't meet Val's eyes.

"They think that dragon got your brother, right?"

"Yeah, but I don't think so. Rowan may be a chicken, but he's a smart chicken, and he wouldn't give himself the opportunity to be eaten."

"Doesn't it feel like the human killer is just one step ahead of us all the time? It sounds like last year you thought you got him. Twice. And he's still out there. Is it possible there's more than one?"

Aspen shrugged. "Maybe. Especially after the death in Hawaii."

"Do you think this has anything to do with the prophecy?"

"What makes you think that?" Aspen asked with a cock of her head.

"Well, the prophecy said that species would fight against species. This is the way the humans are getting involved. Plus, look at the hawks. Why did they attack me? Didn't Sid say hawks attacked his dad as well? That was when he was tracking the human killer. There has to be a connection." Val could feel the pieces fitting together in his head, but parts were still missing. He didn't have all the information he needed.

"You're right. We've been looking at this wrong. Maybe everything is linked. Maybe the war's already started. We need to brainstorm this more with Sid when he gets home. I think you may be onto something. Perhaps if we start looking for connections, we'll find them. Maybe Rowan's disappearance isn't even part of all this."

"So if the war has already started, that means it's even more imperative that I take a queen, right?"

"Yep. You are poor weak dragons without us." She gave a small chuckle.

"So what are we going to do about your sister?"

"What do you mean?"

"How can I take her as my queen if she's avoiding me?" He glanced down at the phone again. "And who the hell is Paul?" Jealousy rose in his chest. He should be the one taking her out to dinner. Not this Paul guy.

"Paul was her boyfriend in high school."

Val didn't like the sound of that. If she was running around with Paul then she wouldn't need him.

"I thought you said she didn't date after Theo."

"Oh, she dated, she just never committed to anyone. Paul was around more than most, but she went out every weekend with different guys. I'm pretty sure she kept that up in Hawaii. When I went with her to the beach to see her surf, there were no less than five guys who all seemed to be enamored with her. She keeps guys at a distance, but they all think they can break through her barrier. I sure hope you can, or we're all in trouble."

"Why?" Val asked.

"Sid has me, and that means he has all the power of all the dragons. But you don't have any of the gifts of the other dragons, and you won't get them without Hazel."

"What?" Val asked. Sid explained a little of this earlier, but he was still unclear on the details.

"You mean you don't know how the bonding ceremony works? You're a dragon."

"It's different for the king," Theo said.

"Oh. I just assumed," Aspen said.

"The gifting happens occasionally when a dragon is bonded with someone not of their race. They take on the gifts of the other one, but only the king has all of them, and he gets them from his queen," said Theo.

Val sat back and ran his hand through his hair. "Are you saying I'll get all the gifts from the dragons?" Holy hell. The implications of that were huge. To have the ability to read minds, judge the feelings around him, and even heal.

Aspen nodded. "Except longevity, as Winerva hasn't been replaced yet. I thought Sid was going to talk to Olwen, but then Rowan got kidnapped, and all plans went out the window."

"I'll talk to Olwen while I'm up there," said Theo.

"Who's Olwen?" Val asked.

"He's the arctic dragon who pledged loyalty to Sid. He could possibly be our only ally in this."

"Oh, good. Then Sid can have a full council again." Aspen twirled her hair, staring off into space.

"So what can you do?" Val asked, hoping she'd tell him more.

"Well, you saw that I can heal. I can speak any language fluently. The other day there was a volunteer who was helping out in the search for Rowan. He's from Russia and only spoke a little English. I had an entire conversation with him without even realizing I was speaking another language. Scared the crap outta me."

"What else?"

"Let's see. Supposedly I can lift heavy things, hide from people when I don't want to be seen. Oh, and I can read minds. But I never use that. I keep it shut off."

"Seems like that would make you a good spy."

"Probably. But for now, I will keep it tucked away. I don't want to know what other people are thinking."

Personally Val thought that would be a nice gift to have. If he knew what Hazel was thinking, then maybe he'd have an easier time winning her over.

CHAPTER 13

H AZEL'S PHONE chirped. She rubbed her eyes and picked it up.

Where the hell are you?

Hazel grinned. Aspen pulled no punches. *None of your business. Where the hell are you?* She loved Aspen more than just about anyone else. Especially because Aspen could say anything to her, and she wouldn't be offended.

At home. Mom said you didn't come home last night.

Hazel looked at the time and then at the sleeping man next to her. She had to admit last night was nice. She was used to waking up next to different men, but since she didn't spend more than a few weeks with them, they never hit the comfortable stage. Paul was comfortable.

It's only six-thirty. Why are you up so early?

Because I haven't seen my sister since August, and I wanted to spend time with her.

Hazel's stomach clenched. She wondered if Aspen had been thinking similar things as her. Right now, she only had one sibling, and she didn't want to take that for granted. No. She couldn't think those thoughts. Rowan was alive.

Give me thirty minutes, and I'll be there. Don't leave.

I might. Mom's driving me crazy already.

Hazel set the phone down and rolled over. Paul was still out. She felt a tinge of guilt for staying with him. He would expect her to act like they were dating again, but if she were being honest with herself, she did it to drive away thoughts of Val.

She couldn't get his face out of her head. Or his voice. Or his smell. She was a lost cause. Paul was sweet, but the whole time they were together, she was thinking of Val.

He blinked his eyes open, smiled, and placed his hand on her cheek. "I've missed you."

She gave him what she hoped looked like a genuine smile.

"I have to go. Aspen's at home waiting. Can you drive me?"

"Of course. What time did you want to do dinner tonight?"

The poor guy. This was so unfair to him. "I'm spending the day with Aspen."

"Oh, well, then, what time will you be back? We can watch a movie or something. I don't care how late it is."

Hazel slid out of bed and talked without looking at him. She couldn't do this staring into his eyes. "Paul, you know this doesn't mean anything. I have to stay focused on the search for Rowan, and then I'm going back to Hawaii. I appreciate you carting me around yesterday." She turned and faced him. He needed to see she was serious. "And last night was wonderful, but it can't happen again. I don't want to get wrapped up in anything that will distract me."

He frowned. "That's okay. I can wait. Maybe I can put in a transfer to Hawaii."

Hazel grabbed his hand. "No, Paul, this isn't going to work. I'm not looking for anything serious."

He sat up and pulled her closer to him. "Maybe not now. But someday you will, and I want to be that person you finally settle down with."

She crawled across the bed and kissed him gently on the lips. "Tell you what. When I decide I'm ready to get married and have babies, you'll be the first one I call."

He gave her a grin and her stomach fell, thoughts not on him, but Val.

Hazel entered the house and heard raised voices. They weren't yelling, but it wasn't a happy conversation. In the kitchen she found her mom and Aspen.

"We need to expand the search."

Mom put her hand on Aspen's. "Look, the car was found in Yellowstone. He's not somewhere else."

"He might be. Come on. Let me at least explore other possibilities."

Hazel took the seat next to Aspen.

"Sweetie, all the evidence points to him being here. We found the car on the road here. He's not somewhere else," said Dad.

Aspen crossed her arms. "You can't know that." Hazel agreed with her sister, but she kept her mouth shut because Aspen was better at convincing them of things than she was.

Mom sat back and sighed. "Well, where do you think he is?"

Aspen threw up her hands. "Who knows? But we'll never know if we don't at least try. He has a better chance at being alive if he's not in the woods."

Hazel's chest tightened at that thought. If Rowan really never left the park, then his chances of survival at this point were slim to none.

Mom rubbed her eyes. "I want to believe you, but I can't. Not when all the evidence says otherwise. Give me one good piece of evidence, and we'll expand the search."

Aspen deflated. "It's just a feeling."

Hazel put her arm around Aspen's shoulder. "I agree with Aspen. For all we know he got in a car with someone else and took off." Hazel hated the idea that they were giving up. It was too soon.

"If he was in the park, the chance that he's alive isn't good," said Aspen.

Dad nodded. "I know, but we want to search around the hot springs and geysers again. If he's not there, then the dragon probably got him." Dad's voice cracked.

Hazel stood up straighter. "There is absolutely nothing that proves he's dead. Doesn't this dragon usually leave a limb or something lying around?"

Mom shook her head. "In the early deaths, he did. But he's getting better. The last three deaths we had were only known because of cameras or eyewitnesses.

Your father and I are holding out hope that he's holed up somewhere, but they are looking for evidence the dragon ate him."

"Fine. Then I'll just continue my own investigation. Aspen, will you help me?"

Aspen nodded, her lips in a tight line. Hazel was glad she could count on her.

Mom stood. "Stay close to town. Take Paul with you. I don't want you girls disappearing. We could really use your help in searching around the hot springs."

"No, I don't want Paul babysitting me. And no, we're not going to search the hot springs. You have enough people looking. I think he's somewhere else."

Mom swept from the room. Probably to go cry. She never cried in front of them. Hazel wanted to feel sorry for her, but she was still angry they weren't exploring other options.

"At least we're on the same page," Aspen said.

"Yeah. Where do you think he is?"

"No idea. But he's not dead."

"I talked to Mr. Daniels, and he said you'd already been there."

Aspen looked down and fiddled with empty cereal bowl. She was keeping a secret from Hazel.

"Yeah. He didn't give us much."

"You know something. I can tell when you are hiding something."

Aspen looked up and met her eyes. "He's not dead."

"So where is he then?"

Aspen sighed. "Don't know. But I want to head to Florida and ask some questions."

Hazel narrowed her eyes. "What makes you think Florida?"

"Because that's where Skye's from."

"You said he wasn't with Skye." Hazel wasn't sure what was going on.

"Oh, he's not. At least I don't think so. But Skye might know where he went. She was closer to him than any of us at the moment he disappeared. I guess there's the possibility that he ran off with her, but probably not."

Hazel sat down. She didn't think anything would surprise her at this point. Rowan was always a nerdy kid who never even talked to girls. To think that he ran off with one was more unbelievable than getting eaten by a dragon.

"Let me guess, you tried to tell Mom and Dad, and they didn't believe you," Hazel said.

"Uh, no. I didn't tell them."

"Why not? This could change everything." Hazel grew more confused by the second.

"It's complicated. I'm only telling you because I need you on my side, but you can't tell them either."

Hazel sighed. "Aspen, I know in your head you've worked out why we can't tell them and that we'll just find him on our own, but this is serious. We need to tell our parents and alert the authorities."

"We can't."

"Why?" Bringing in the FBI was the best chance they had at finding him. They had resources that she and Aspen wouldn't have.

"Because of Sid's family. I told you it was complicated."

"What does any of this have to do with Sid's family?"

Aspen looked at the stairs. "Mom might come back down at any minute. Let's go for a drive."

Hazel tried to sort out her thoughts as they went outside. She stopped short when she saw Aspen unlock the doors of an Escalade.

"That's not your car."

"Mine's still in the shop. Sid's sick of my car breaking down, and he's buying me a new one. In the meantime, I'm driving this thing. Come on."

Hazel tried to wrap her head around Aspen having a boyfriend who was going to buy her a new car. This one was all decked out. Aspen leaned over and switched on the heated seats.

"Nice, huh?"

"Yeah. Now talk. I wanna know more about Skye."

Aspen backed out of the driveway and headed into town. She laughed. "Skye's Sid's ex-girlfriend and the one that he was supposed to be with. I threw a damper into all their plans."

Hazel frowned. "I think you need to back up a little."

"There are things I can't tell you. Things you'll learn eventually but for now should be kept secret, so if there are holes in my story, that's why."

"Nope. You can't do that. You need to tell me everything if we are going to find Rowan."

"Sis, it's not my secret to share. If you want to know the things I'm leaving out, you need to ask Val. I imagine he'll tell you. But I'll tell you everything I can."

"What's Val got do with any of this?" So much for staying away from him. If he had answers, she'd have to talk to him. Unless she could convince Aspen to give her the answers first.

"I told you, he's Sid's cousin. And this whole mess is because of Sid's family."

"Alright, start at the beginning."

"Sid moved here while we were in Hawaii, and when we got back, he and I hit it off. His family has a lot of money, and I was not in the plans. He wasn't supposed to hook up with anyone while he was here.

In fact, your buddy Teddy told me one time that Sid was not supposed to be with anyone, and then asked me to get lost. A month later Skye showed up and helped us keep our relationship secret. For a while we pretended that they were a couple, and Sid and I only really saw each other in the privacy of his home. Rowan came along for the ride, and he and Skye spent a lot of time together."

"I never would've thought Rowan would run away with a girl."

Aspen laughed. "Wait until you see a picture of her. Then you really won't believe it. Seriously though, they probably aren't together. But Skye might have information."

"Has anyone seen Skye?"

"Nope."

"What makes you so sure they aren't together?"

"Because Skye wasn't looking to get involved with anyone. She had no reason to run away and take Rowan with her. She'd know we would think a dragon ate him. She wouldn't put us through that. But if she doesn't know he's missing, she might not know she has information that could help us find him."

"Were they a couple?"

Aspen laughed. "No. I always told Rowan he was fighting a losing battle, but near the end it was hard to tell. She seemed to really like him. Rowan thought he had a shot."

"Why isn't anyone worried about Skye missing?"

"Because Skye disappears from time to time, and apparently it isn't that big of a deal. But she was the last one who saw him before he disappeared."

"What makes you think that?"

"Because Mr. Daniels said a blonde girl was driving the car."

"And Skye is blonde?"

Aspen grinned. "Very. A knockout too."

"So how are we going to find her?"

"We're not. Sid and his family will take care of it. I trust he'll find Skye."

"But you just said we were going to Florida."

"No, I said I wanted to. We'll help field intel. But we're not leaving Gardiner. There is one more thing you should know. And I don't want you to freak out."

Hazel clenched her fists. She wasn't sure she'd be able to take any more. "I'm past freaking out."

"There is a small possibility that they are together but didn't run away."

"You just said they weren't together." Hazel voice raised a few octaves. She was about ready to throttle Aspen for being so cryptic.

"No, I said they probably weren't together. This is the other part."

Hazel raised an eyebrow. "What do you mean?"

"A family feud is starting. There are a lot of puzzle pieces, but the more research we do, the more we realize that they may all be connected. Including Rowan's disappearance. They might have been kidnapped."

"What?" Hazel's voice came out in a squeak. "We've got to go to the FBI."

"No, we can't. They won't help us with this."

Hazel was baffled. Why on earth would her sister want to hide something that could help them find Rowan? She was being completely unreasonable.

"Are they some kind of mafia or something?" Hazel couldn't imagine what would make her sister keep something this big a secret.

Aspen shook her head. "No, look, I'm going to let Sid and Val explain. We're going to help in the search, but we can't tell Mom or anyone else."

"Why did you tell me?"

"Because you deserve to be part of this."

Aspen pulled onto Shelby Lane, and Hazel's stomach twisted for a very different reason.

"Do we really have to go here?" Val would be there. She had to focus on Rowan. She couldn't risk Val distracting her. Memories of that kiss haunted her more than she liked to admit. She desperately wanted a repeat, but knew that would be foolish.

"That was my first reaction too." Aspen laughed.

Hazel looked quizzically at her. "Why's that?"

"Sid looks just like Marc. Found out they were cousins. But he's dead now, so it doesn't matter."

"This just gets weirder and weirder." She wanted to slow down, process everything her sister was telling her, but they arrived at the house, and Hazel knew the stories would have to wait.

"You have no idea, Sis. But don't worry. Theo isn't here. He's out of town."

Hazel got out of the car and stared up at the monster house. "It's not Teddy I'm worried about."

Aspen nudged her and grinned. "I like Val. He really likes you too."

"You would like him." Hazel snorted.

"What's that supposed to mean?"

"He's all batty about dragons. He told me on the airplane." If Aspen wasn't already with Sid, she'd be worried about her sister making a move on Val. Maybe she would anyway. Hazel wasn't sure if she liked or loathed that idea. If Aspen went after him, then she'd be able to write him off.

Aspen leaned against the car. "What happened on the airplane anyway? Val seems pretty in love."

Hazel smiled in spite of herself. If Val was talking about her, then Aspen wasn't going to even consider him. "We talked the whole plane ride. It's not a big deal."

Aspen wiggled her eyebrows. "Did you kiss him?"

Hazel blushed and didn't say anything.

"Yeah, nice. He's excited to see you again, but he won't be back for a couple of hours. The boys wanted to give us some time to talk."

Hazel followed Aspen into the house. She shut the door, and something flew right at her head, and she ducked, covering her head.

She peeked through her hands. A strange creature sat on Aspen's shoulder.

Aspen was looking at the little critter with exasperation. "Runa, I told you not to come out until Hazel went home."

The creature stuck her tongue out at Aspen and spoke. "Since when have I listened to you? She's got green eyes too."

Hazel sunk to the floor, a little lightheaded. Her head raced to understand. But nothing made sense.

"What is that?" It looked like a giant lizard with wings. But was all sorts of crazy colors. Maybe she didn't get enough sleep the night before. She closed her eyes for a second then opened them again. Nope the creature was still there.

The lizard hopped off Aspen's shoulder and stuck her snout in Hazel's face. Hazel backed away.

"I'm a dragon." It cocked its head from side to side. Maybe it would open its mouth and incinerate her. Her confusion turned to fear, and her palms began to sweat.

"Why is it talking?" Hazel fought to keep from stuttering. Her chest was tight, and her breath was coming in rapid bursts.

The little dragon jerked its head back and looked at Aspen. "Did she just call me an it?"

Aspen shrugged. "Sorry."

She had to be hallucinating. There was no other explanation. Maybe it was the combination of lack of sleep and bad coffee. Perhaps her mom had goofed and somehow spiked her coffee like she did for Rowan when he was having a panic attack. Medicines like that could cause hallucinations. Couldn't they? Once again, Hazel squeezed her eyes shut and hoped that when she opened them, the dragon would be gone. But she wasn't that lucky. She made eye contact, and it puffed its chest out and stretched its neck high.

"I can talk because I'm part river dragon."

"Do they all talk?" Hazel squeaked, still not sure what was going on. She took a couple of deep breaths and tried to process what she knew about dragons. It wasn't much. Maybe only river dragons could talk.

"Of course. Everyone knows that." The dragon turned her head back to Aspen. "Your sister isn't very smart. Why does Val like her?"

Hazel kept her body pressed against the wall. "Why's it talking about Val?"

"Runa, you've scared her. Can you go back to your room until I explain some things to my sister?"

"Rowan was supposed to be afraid of everything, and he wasn't scared of me."

Hazel leaned forward, both fascinated and horrified by the dragon in front of her. She was real. Not a hallucination. Her skin was a mottle of many different colors, and she had bright yellow wings. Hazel wanted to touch her skin, to see what it felt like, but the dragon turned around and narrowed her eyes.

"Why are you scared of me?"

"Because an animal just spoke to me. I don't know many speaking animals, do you?"

"Sure, they all do. Only most do it with their minds."

"You've said enough. Room. Now."

Runa huffed and spread out her wings and took flight. She hit Aspen right on the head as she flew down the hall. Aspen rubbed her head and held her hand out for Hazel.

"Sorry about her. I'd hoped to explain a few things before she showed her face."

Hazel took Aspen's hand and pulled herself up. "Is she your pet or something?"

Aspen laughed. "Runa is no one's pet. She's just staying with us for a while. She doesn't want to go back home."

"Why not?"

"Her father kept her locked up in a cave."

"Sounds cruel." Hazel was trying to wrap her head around the fact that dragons could talk. That they were able to make decisions like humans.

"Oh, it's not. Most underground dragons go blind in the light of day, but because she's part river dragon, she can come out. She stowed away with me when Sid and I came back from DC last year. We don't have the heart to send her home."

None of what Aspen said made sense, so Hazel grabbed onto the one thing that she understood. "When did you go to DC?"

Aspen gave her a crooked grin. "That is part of much larger story. You ready to have your mind blown?"

"I just met a talking dragon. I don't think you could surprise me even more."

Aspen snorted. "Famous last words."

"Come on, let's go into the theater room. It's the most comfortable. Sid and Val will be back in a couple of hours, and we'll eat. They can tell you everything, but now that you've met Runa, I can tell you about the dragons."

Hazel tried to watch where she was going as she walked down the hall, but there was so much to look at. Every few feet there was another old painting, and ancient-looking statues filled every cubby. She'd never been anywhere so opulent.

She pointed to a picture as Aspen opened a door. "Are these authentic?"

"I think so. But art has never been my thing. I didn't think it was yours either."

Hazel leaned forward and studied the red and black painting. "It's not, but I took an art history class last semester. This looks like Picasso."

"You'll have to ask Sid. I have no idea."

Hazel followed Aspen into the room. It was dark, cozy, and comfortable. Aspen flung herself down on the massive couch, and Hazel followed, facing her sister.

"It's time for you to explain." Hazel was tired of having way more questions than she had the answers to. She wasn't used to being left in the dark.

Aspen hesitated. "Sid and his family are liaisons between the dragon world and the human one. It's why we went to DC. We had to meet with the president to talk about the dragon killings."

Hazel gasped. "You met with the president?" She had truly thought nothing else would surprise her. But every time Aspen opened her mouth, she said something unimaginable.

Aspen grinned. "Yeah, I told her off too."

Hazel shook her head. "Only you would do that. Why?"

"She talked about nuking the dragon homes."

"A lot of people think they should. The dragons are too dangerous to keep around."

Aspen face went red, and she motioned toward the door. "Did Runa look too dangerous to keep around?"

"She's tiny, and she can talk. I still can't believe she can talk." Hazel knew she was making Aspen angry, but at this point she didn't care. She wanted answers, and she'd get them even if she and Aspen weren't speaking by the time this was over.

"They're intelligent beings. They all can communicate."

Hazel had to think on that. Those massive flying beasts could communicate with humans?

"Wait. Paul said he saw you riding a black dragon. I thought he was just seeing things. But it's true, isn't it?"

"Yeah. I've befriended a lot of them, but the black one is my favorite."

Hazel backed away from Aspen, reality setting in. Her heart beat a little faster. "They're eating people."

"No, only one dragon is eating people. Believe it or not, the dragons want to find him as bad as we do. We shouldn't kill them all just because one of them is evil. They'll find him, and things will all go back to normal."

"No it won't. You can't just unknow this stuff."

Aspen laid her hand on Hazel's. "It gets better. I promise. Look, I was shocked when I found all this out too. Now it doesn't faze me."

"But you've always liked dragons. I don't."

Aspen was probably giddy as all get out when she discovered the dragons could talk to her.

"Rowan didn't either, and he got used to the idea. He and Runa were good buddies."

"Where is he?"

"Runa is a she, not a he."

"Not Runa, Rowan." Aspen had to know more than she was letting on.

"No idea. But there's a war starting among the dragons, and it's possible that someone kidnapped Skye because of it. The other thing that complicates things is that she told me she was going to go into hiding just before she left."

"What does Skye have to do with the dragons?"

"She's part of all this liaison stuff."

"Why'd she want to go into hiding in the first place?"

"Because she thought she was going to die. It's a long story, and it involves secrets I can't tell you."

"But then why didn't she just leave? She drove Rowan into the park." Hazel was trying to see how everything was connected. Nothing was adding up.

"Why would she involve Rowan? Skye cared about him. She wouldn't want him caught up in this mess," Aspen said.

"Maybe she was just bringing Rowan home." Hazel wanted to find some sense in this. But Aspen left out too many details.

"That seems unlikely as he never made it home." Aspen seemed just as confused as Hazel was.

"Are you sure about that? Did anyone search his room?"

Aspen laughed. "He's not hiding in his room."

"I know that, but there may be clues, if he did make it home first."

"The car was found on the road."

"He could've walked home. Did anyone search his room?"

"I assume Mom and Dad did, but maybe not. If they saw the broken down jeep and just assumed he was taken by the dragon, they wouldn't even think to check his room."

Hazel sank onto the couch. "If they'd just gotten the FBI involved right away, they would've done this right. But now we're dealing with things that are a week old. How are we going to find him?" It felt like everyone just assumed he was dead even if they didn't admit it. Like there was no other explanation except the almighty human-eating dragon.

"We're doing everything we can."

"What if Skye kidnapped him?"

Aspen burst out laughing. Hazel crossed her arms and glared at her. "Look, I'm sorry. But Skye wouldn't hurt a fly. She's as harmless as they come."

"Whatever, I want to go home and check Rowan's room."

Aspen leaned over to the ottoman next to the couch and scooped out a handful of M&Ms from a bowl. "You want some?"

Hazel shook her head. "No, seriously, I want to go home."

"You have to wait. I promised Sid and Val we'd eat with them. Then I'll take you home. They're bringing takeout."

Hazel let out a breath. "I'm not hungry, and I don't want to see Val."

Aspen giggled. "Why? Because you like him?"

Hazel forgot how perceptive Aspen was. "Maybe. But I can't get involved. Not with Rowan out there. Especially now that you said he might be kidnapped."

Aspen's phone buzzed. "They're here. Come on, let's eat, and then we'll decide what to do about Rowan."

Hazel wasn't sold on the idea, but she didn't have any other choice. She'd been worried before that Rowan was dead, and now she had to worry that a few murderous dragons were holding him captive. She wasn't sure which was worse.

CHAPTER 14

VAL WIPED HIS sweaty hands on his jeans. He'd never been so nervous before. Sid grabbed the bag of food from the backseat.

"You okay?" Sid asked.

"Uh, no. She said she never wanted to see me again."

"Look, Aspen hated me when we first met. At least you know Hazel likes you. You'll be fine. Just relax and act like you did on the airplane."

Val nodded, still worried. "Explain again Aspen's cover story for us."

"We're a family that acts as liaisons for the dragons. You and I are third cousins, and we're leading the search for the human killer."

"What'd she tell her about the mark?" That was the one thing they didn't cover in the conversation at the restaurant while they waited for their food.

"If they talked about it at all, Aspen was going to play dumb. Tell her that it had to do with the dragons, but the dragons wouldn't tell her what."

"What if she doesn't want to see me?" Val had never been so insecure in his life.

Sid put his hand on Val's shoulder. "Relax. It will be fine. Seriously. Look, if she's trying to avoid you, then you need to do something for her that no one else can so that she has to turn to you. With Aspen, I introduced her to myself in dragon form because that's what she wanted. What does Hazel want?"

"To find Rowan."

"There's your answer. Offer to help her search. If Aspen's right and Skye and Rowan were kidnapped, you can help her find clues. Be sneaky about it if you have to. Act like you aren't supposed to involve her. It will gain her trust."

Val followed Sid into the house, and they set out the food. Val had no idea what it was, but it smelled good.

Aspen bounced into the room and slid her arm around Sid's waist before giving him a quick kiss on the lips. "Did you get me orange chicken?"

"Sure did. But you have to share this time."

She snatched the box out of Sid's hand and grabbed a pair of sticks off the table. "Nope, this is all mine."

Val envied the easy way in which they bantered.

"And mine," squawked Runa as she flew into the room and landed on the counter behind Aspen and stuck her head in the box.

Aspen jerked the box away. "Hey, get off."

"But it's my favorite." Runa had a smear of orange sauce on the bottom of her jaw.

"Go to the table, missy."

Val had been so distracted by Aspen and Runa that he hadn't seen Hazel. But as she quietly slid into a chair across the table, his eyes met hers, and she gave him a tight smile.

He took the rest of the boxes and spread them out. He sat next to Hazel but didn't look at her. Instead, he looked at Aspen, who was using the sticks to eat her food while trying to keep it out of the mouth of Runa.

Val picked up another pair of sticks and turned to Hazel. "How do we eat with these?"

Her face softened. "I forgot you grew up in a very sheltered home. I suppose you haven't used chopsticks. Here, let me show you."

She picked up another pair of sticks and arranged them in her fingers so she was able to pick a piece of chicken out of another box. Val tried to copy her, but one stick fell right out of his hand.

Hazel laughed softly, and his heart fluttered. "Watch the chopsticks," she said and pointed back at her hand.

She held his hand and moved his fingers so they held the chopsticks the way she had. He shivered at her touch and looked over at her, but her eyes were on his fingers.

"Look, hold this one tight and don't let it move. Hold the other one loosely and use your index finger to move it."

She pushed down on his index finger and showed him how the stick would move up and down. She removed her hand, and he immediately dropped them. Probably because he was watching her face instead of their hands.

"Oops. I wasn't ready for you to let go."

"Try again." She handed him the sticks, and he took them from her, making sure he brushed the back of her hand with his fingertips. She frowned for a second but then recovered. "See if you can do it."

He tried to position them in his hand like she did, but they wouldn't work. She moved his fingers around, and he was able to move the top stick up and down. But as soon as he reached for a piece of food, they went all wonky again.

Sid laughed. "Guess you aren't getting any food tonight."

"Yeah, watch me." Val sat one of the sticks down and stabbed a piece of chicken with the other one. "See, I can still eat."

Aspen pulled a fork out of a drawer and handed it to him before she sat down.

"Don't let Sid fool you. He only got the hang of them a few weeks ago."

Hazel looked between the both of them. "Did you have a sheltered upbringing too?"

Sid shrugged. "I guess you could say that. We never had Chinese takeout when I was growing up. But I wasn't isolated on an island like Val."

Val and Sid had discussed the differences in their upbringing the night before. Val envied that Sid was actually given some preparation for the kingship, thought he was glad he wasn't the only one who didn't know how to use chopsticks.

Hazel was quiet during dinner. Aspen and Sid teased each other quite a bit. Val wanted to reach over and grab Hazel's hand, but he was afraid of her reaction. He decided to start with a question.

"Did Aspen tell you about us?" he said and pointed to Sid and himself.

"You mean that you are liaisons or something for the dragons?"

"Yeah. I'm sure you have questions."

She took a bite of food and pursed her lips. "All that stuff you said on the airplane about being an orphan and never being off the island, was that just a story?"

"Oh no. That was all true. I grew up among the dragons. Aside from my family, I had very little human interaction. It's why I sometimes don't understand what things are."

"Why come here? Is your father really here?"

"Yes, he is. And I'm also helping with the search for the human killer. The dragons need us to communicate for them." Val thought he was doing a pretty good job sticking to the story. Hazel seemed convinced at least. It helped that most of it was the actual truth.

"Can you talk to the dragons?" She leaned closer to him, and he inhaled her sweet scent.

Runa piped up. "You can talk to me. Why are you asking him if he can talk to dragons?"

Hazel narrowed her eyes. "But you said not all dragons could talk."

Val interjected. "That is true, but they all can communicate. Mostly through their minds."

Aspen glanced over at Hazel. "It's true. I talk to my black dragon all the time. Rowan's done it too."

Hazel squeezed her eyes shut. "I don't think I'm going to ask any more questions. I don't like the answers I get."

Val let her be after that. He didn't want to push her. When she was ready, she'd ask.

After dinner Hazel and Val helped Sid and Aspen all throw away the containers. He wanted to stay close to her.

"I should go. I want to check out Rowan's room." Hazel pushed her chair away from the table and stood up.

Aspen slid closer to Sid. "I'm not leaving yet. Give me a couple hours, and I'll take you home. Promise. Really, you're not going to find anything in there. He didn't go home first."

Hazel picked up Aspen's keys from the counter. "Says you. And Aspen, you said you'd take me home after we ate. Come on."

Aspen pouted. "One hour."

Sid looked at Val and mouthed, "You're welcome."

Val appreciated Sid's thoughtfulness at giving him more time with Hazel, but he didn't think she'd give up that quick.

"I'll take you home," he said.

Aspen started laughing. "You haven't learned how to drive yet. Remember?"

"Oh, yeah," he said, looking at his shoes, embarrassed.

"Look, if you can provide the car, I can drive. I'll bring it back tomorrow," Hazel said and crossed her arms.

Val looked up. "Can I come with you? I haven't seen much of the area yet, and I'd like to go for a drive." She'd probably say no, but it was worth a shot.

Hazel studied him for a second before she finally said, "Sure. I want to come back here and talk to Aspen about what I find anyway."

Sid rummaged around a drawer and then threw her a set of keys. "This has keys for all the cars in there. It's supposed to snow, so you should probably pick something that has four-wheel drive."

Hazel followed Val out to the garage. She was quiet while she studied the six vehicles. To Val they all looked similar. He didn't understand why one would be better than the other. Finally, she pointed to a truck. "That one."

Hazel hesitated before getting in. "You know, it might be easier if I just go alone."

"I'm pretty good at searching for things. Maybe I'll spot something that you don't. Come on. I want to see more of the area. I promise I'll be helpful."

She sighed but then nodded and unlocked the doors.

He sat in the passenger seat, and Hazel climbed up in the driver's seat.

"Do you have a license?" Hazel asked as she pulled out of the driveway.

"Yeah. Obviously, I didn't earn it. But Theo gave me one in Hawaii. Along with a whole bunch of paperwork I didn't know I needed. I still have no idea what a voter registration card is."

Hazel hesitated for a second. "Yeah, you probably won't use that. Do you want to learn how?"

"To drive?" Val shrugged. He figured he wouldn't be around long enough to really need to. Once he found his queen, they'd live among the dragons. Especially considering that they had a war to fight. "Too much going on right now to think about driving."

Hazel sighed. "You got that right. Do you think Rowan was kidnapped?"

"I don't know."

"I want to find him. To make sure he's okay. That's all."

Val looked over and saw a tear slide down her cheek, and his stomach hurt for her. He unbuckled his seatbelt and slid close to her.

He brushed away her tears. "Hey, don't cry. We'll find him. I'll help you."

She snorted. "Yeah, right. You'd probably just slow me down."

He clenched his fists. "What makes you think that?"

"Because you aren't vested in the search at all. Plus, you can't even drive. I'll be better off on my own. But I might bring Paul with me after tonight. You'll just get in the way."

"Who's Paul?" Val knew this already, but he wanted to hear her story.

Her lips twitched. "He's an old boyfriend from school. He's in the National Guard, so he can get me into places I couldn't otherwise. I'll have to talk to him after I drop you off."

Jealously bloomed in Val's chest, and he moved away from Hazel before he did something stupid, like try to kiss her while she was driving.

"What about…"

"Us?" Hazel finished for him. She stopped at an intersection and looked right at him with a seriousness she didn't have two seconds ago. "I told you before I don't do commitment. Honestly, I was hoping I'd never see you again."

Pain knifed through his chest. "You're saying that kiss meant nothing?"

Hazel frowned, confusion etched on her features.

"Look, I, Val…I can't explain it. I didn't mean to hurt you, but I can't be with you."

Val closed the distance again, but he didn't touch her. "There's absolutely no reason for us not to be together."

"Yeah, there is." She pushed against his chest. "You need to buckle your seatbelt."

He did as she asked, and she continued down the road. Val wasn't going to let her get away without explaining. "What's that? Please explain it to me because I don't get it. Do you find me repulsive?"

Hazel pulled into her driveway. She put the car into park and looked over at him. "I like you. A lot. But my life is complicated, and your life is complicated, and I just don't want to get involved with anyone."

Val racked his brain. He had no idea how he was going to win her over. She didn't say anything else as they walked up to the house. It was much smaller than Sid's but had a wide front porch. Hazel let herself in.

"Are your parents home?" he asked, following her in.

She shook her head. "They're at work. They've started the second search of the park." Then she headed up a set of stairs.

They walked up the stairs and into a small bedroom. The bed was neatly made up, but aside from the large television on the wall, a dresser, and a fairly empty bookshelf, the room was empty.

Hazel opened a few drawers, and Val looked in the closet. He didn't see anything out of the ordinary. A few button-up shirts hung on hangers, and on the floor of the closet sat two pairs of shoes.

"Do you see a suitcase in the top of the closet?" Hazel asked.

"No. There's nothing up there. His drawers?"

"Mostly empty."

Val shut the door and sat on the bed. "Pretty inconclusive, huh?"

Hazel sank down next to him. "His suitcase is gone, and his drawers are empty. I'd say he ran away. But Aspen said I can't tell my parents what's going on. I don't understand why. Plus according to Aspen, there is the possibility that he was kidnapped with that Skye chick."

Val put his hand over hers, and since she didn't remove it, he left it there. "Look, our family is pretty messed up. Maybe he was taken, and maybe he ran on his own. Tell you what, why don't we go to Florida and see if we can find any information on Skye. Maybe someone's seen her. If she's not with him, she might have at least seen him."

"Aspen said they've been trying to find her."

"Just dragons or eagles acting on orders. They didn't have your need to know. Come on. I'll take you."

She stood and paced the room. Val wanted to know what she was thinking, but he let her be.

Finally, she sat down and put her hand on his cheek. "Val, I'm scared."

He barely heard her words, completely surprised by her sudden affection. All he could think about was her hand on his face. "Of what?" he asked.

She crossed her arms and looked out the window as she spoke.

"Of this, of us. Of falling in love. Teddy hurt me so badly. I can't go through that again. When he left, I thought for sure I'd never be happy again. Paul let me see I could be in a relationship without love. He's easy. I can get him to take me to Florida. Aspen will tell us where to go. You'll just distract me."

She wrung her hands and wouldn't look at him. Val wanted her to keep talking to figure out her innermost thoughts. "You know, keeping everyone at a distance must feel pretty empty."

She laughed. "That's the thing. It's not. I'm happy. I enjoy my life and my flings. I don't want the intensity of a serious relationship. Because I can't handle the aftermath when it inevitably falls apart."

Val stood close to her. He took both of her hands in his and looked deep into her eyes. "I have never felt this way about anyone before. I love you."

Hazel let out a loud laugh and ripped her hands from him. She backed away, crossed her arms, and raised an eyebrow.

"You've been taking lessons from Teddy, huh?"

"What are you talking about?" His face flushed. He'd just opened up to her, and she shot him down.

"Teddy used those *exact* same words the day before he disappeared."

"I didn't…I don't even talk to Theo. I meant them." One of these days he was going to beat the crap out of Theo for what he did to Hazel. But first Val had to convince her he wasn't like him.

"Yeah, that's what he said too. This isn't going to work. You'll break my heart, and I don't think it can survive that again. I'll take you home, and then I'll call Paul to take me to Florida."

She ran from the room. He didn't follow. He'd opened up too soon, and now she would keep him at arm's length. Not only that, but he'd run her right back to that idiot Paul. Dammit. He wished someone had taught him how to do this. Because he was blowing it big time. Some king he would be. He couldn't even get the future queen who'd already sealed herself to him to love him.

CHAPTER 15

VAL TOSSED AND turned all night. His bed was comfortable, but he flung his pillows everywhere. Hazel's words kept bouncing around in his head. He didn't know how to show her he wouldn't hurt her. He supposed he could talk about the mark and what it meant. Would that convince her?

He checked his phone throughout the night. One a.m. Two a.m. Four a.m. He finally got up at six.

No one else was up yet. He went into the kitchen, opened the fridge, and pulled out an apple. When he turned around, he was surprised to find a pretty redhead sitting at the kitchen table. She smiled at him.

"You must be Val."

"I am. You are?" He took a bite of the apple, sleep fogging his brain.

"Pearl. Obsidian's sister."

Sid had mentioned his sister was on the council. "What brings you here?"

"Nothing good." She sighed. "I wished I'd lived five hundred years ago instead of now."

"Why?"

"Because everyone I love is going to die." Her face was pale, and her shoulders tight. Val tried to make sense of what she was saying. He wanted to say something that would make her feel better, but he couldn't think of anything real.

Runa came flying into the room. "There you are, Val. I couldn't find you." She landed in front of Pearl. "I woke everyone else up. They'll be down in a minute."

"Thank you," Pearl said and patted Runa on the head.

Runa growled. "I'm not a dog."

Pearl gave her a grin. "I know. I'm sorry."

Within minutes, Sid and Aspen joined them. Val tried to clear the sleep fog from his brain, trying to understand what was going on.

Pearl jumped up and threw her arms around Sid. She quickly let go of him and addressed both Sid and Aspen. Val felt like an intruder. "I was up north with Theo spying on the arctic dragons, and, Sid, I've got bad news."

"What?"

"Olwen is dead."

"What?" Sid whipped his shirt off and ran to the small bathroom off the kitchen. Seconds later, he came back, with his fists clenched.

"What's the matter?" Aspen asked.

"Jolantha is gone as well," Sid said, pointing to his chest.

"What?"

When Sid had transformed as a dragon a few days ago, there had been seven seals on his chest. Now there were only five.

"Does that mean they're being targeted?" Pearl asked.

"Probably. Dammit. I shouldn't have the let the council talk me out of finishing the seals."

"It was necessary. To keep the peace. You didn't want to be the first dragon in thousands of years to take the throne by force when it was freely given," said Pearl.

"Except now the rest of them are in danger."

"Runa's here, so we can keep her safe. We can probably bring your mom and Runa's mom here. Damien will be harder because he's too big for the house and can't transform into a human." Aspen let out a deep breath.

"So what are you going to do for my dad?"

Sid put his hand on Val's shoulder. "We'll get a few royal dragons to stay with him. Don't worry. We'll take care of him."

Val studied the marks on Sid's chest. "What about Skye?"

Sid squeezed his eyes shut. "She'll be a target. An easy one, since she has no idea someone is hunting her."

Aspen crossed her arms. "Unless they've already got her."

"She's still alive though. Or her mark would be gone. Why kill the others but keep her alive?"

Pearl leaned against the counter near Sid. "Information. She knows a lot about you."

"We've got eagles and dragons all over the country looking. There's been no sight of her."

Val thought quickly. Hazel wanted to find Skye just as much as they did. "What if you send me and Hazel to Florida? You've had dragons searching. Maybe you need a couple of humans to see if we can round anything up. Based on what I've seen, Rowan is either dead, or he's with her."

Aspen nodded. "That's a good idea, but I'm going with as well. She won't go alone with you."

Val wanted to object, but he figured she had a point. Sid stared off into space for a few seconds. "That's a decent idea. It's something we haven't tried yet. If they weren't in danger before, they're in danger now."

Aspen hopped down off the counter she'd been sitting on. "I'll go get Hazel. Let's go find my brother."

CHAPTER 16

HAZEL STEPPED OUT of the shower, wrapped herself in a towel, opened the door, and stopped dead. Aspen stood right in front of her.

"What the? Why are you standing outside my door?"

Aspen rocked back on her heels. "We need to go to Florida. Today."

"Why?"

"We have reason to believe that Skye and Rowan, if he's with her, are in danger."

"Why?"

"People like Skye are turning up dead."

"Like Skye?"

Aspen pushed Hazel toward her room. "Skye was pretty tightly woven in the dragon world, like Sid and Val. Two of their family members ended up dead last night. We need to find her."

"What about Sid and Val?"

"They are going to warn the others that are in danger."

Hazel brushed past Aspen to her bedroom. "But aren't they in danger as well? Who wants to hurt them? Why?"

"Sid's family has been in charge of the dragon stuff for a long time, and someone else wants to take over."

Aspen wouldn't meet her eyes. Hazel stepped into her closet to get dressed. Something was off. But Hazel could focus on that, or she could help solve the problem at hand. She could worry about the mystery of Sid and Val's family later.

"Any idea where to start the search?" She pulled a sweatshirt over her head and tried to process this new development.

"Everglades. We'll talk to the rangers. Flash around pictures. Do whatever it takes to find them."

"We need to tell Mom and Dad."

Aspen grabbed Hazel's arm. "We can't."

"What are we going to do, just disappear and let them think we're never coming back either? We need to tell them something."

"Fine, but you can't tell them that Skye or Sid is involved."

Hazel rolled her eyes. "Fair enough. I'll come up with something."

Aspen nodded and followed her downstairs.

Their parents were sitting at the table eating breakfast. Mom looked up. Her eyes were red and her face blotchy.

"The search is over."

Hazel sank into her chair, a knot forming in her chest. "Did they find his body?"

"No, but all hope is lost. He's gone."

Hazel put her hands over her mother's. "Maybe not."

Mom shook her head. "Don't start. He's dead. We need to accept that."

"No, I don't think so. Listen, yesterday I checked his room. His drawers are empty, and his suitcase is missing."

"You think we didn't do a thorough search? We scoured his room the day he disappeared. His suitcase is in the garage. We never put it back after the trip to Hawaii, and he had a lot of clothes in the wash. You're searching for clues that aren't there."

"I have a friend who spotted him in Florida. I think he ran away. I don't know why, and I don't know how, but I want to follow this lead."

Mom narrowed her eyes at Hazel. "That's impossible. You will stay here and help us. We cannot keep chasing irrational leads. He's dead."

Hazel crossed her arms. "Aspen and I are going. We'll be back in a couple of days."

Mom and Dad looked at each other. "No. The funeral is on Tuesday. You're not leaving."

Aspen leaned forward. "We can be home by Tuesday. That only gives us a couple of days to search, but that should be enough."

After a few seconds, Dad sighed. "I don't know about this."

If Dad was speaking, it was a good sign. He usually let Mom be the bad guy, but if they were going to get away with anything, he'd be the one to let them.

"Look, we're going to do this whether you approve or not. You may believe he's dead, but we don't."

Mom squeezed her eyes shut. "You're right. We can't stop you. But promise me something. If you don't find anything out there, will you please try to move on?"

Hazel nodded, hating the lie. But she needed her mom to feel okay about something.

"How are you getting there?" Dad asked.

"Flying. Sid's paying for the tickets."

"Be safe. We'll see you girls on Tuesday morning."

Back at Sid's house, Hazel waited in the foyer for Aspen, who needed to pack up her own things. Sid had booked them on a two o'clock flight. Runa flew into the room.

"Where's Aspen?" Runa hovered in the air in front of her.

"Upstairs packing."

The little dragon turned and flew up the stairs, just as Aspen was coming down them. Aspen was looking at her phone, and Runa was looking at herself in the mirror on the wall. Before Hazel could shout a warning, they collided. The suitcase went flying, and Aspen fell down after it, Runa tumbling with her. Hazel's heart raced as she caught her sister at the bottom.

"Are you okay?"

Aspen rubbed at her head. "I think so." Then she glared at Runa. "You've got to look where you're going."

Runa hung her now red head. "I'm sorry. But in my defense, you weren't looking either."

Aspen rolled her eyes and grabbed Hazel's hand. "Help me up. Change of plans. Skye's been spotted."

"What? Where?"

Hazel hoisted Aspen up, and she immediately collapsed again, her face twisted.

"What's the matter?"

"My ankle. I can't stand on it."

Val came running into the room. "What happened? I heard a crash."

"Aspen fell down the stairs. Let me see your ankle."

It was red and starting to swell. "We need to get you the doctor."

She took a deep breath. "No, I'll be okay. Look, you need to go find Skye. She's in Yosemite."

"Is Rowan with her?"

"I don't know. Our source was looking for Skye, not Rowan."

"Is she okay?"

"Don't know. She was seen hiking. She could be hidden somewhere. You've got to go. Val, go with her. I'll be fine. Sid will be home soon. He can take me the doctor. This is more important."

Val nodded. "I'll be right back."

He ran up the stairs two at a time. Hazel glared at Aspen. "Did you do this on purpose?"

"What, hurt my ankle?"

"Yeah. So I'd have to go with Val."

"What the hell? Do you think I care about your freaking love life? Rowan is out there. Mom and Dad think he's dead, and this is our only lead. I wouldn't joke about this."

"Okay, I'm sorry. I just thought... It seemed contrived, that's all."

Hazel turned away, but just before she did, she could've sworn she saw Runa wink at Aspen.

Hazel helped Aspen into the kitchen where she eased into a chair.

"How bad does it hurt?" Hazel asked.

Aspen grimaced. "I could use some ibuprofen."

Hazel dug around in her bag. "Of course. Here." Hazel hated seeing her sister in pain. Aspen was always strong and moved forward with what seemed like superhuman strength. To see her hurt was disconcerting.

Runa settled on the kitchen table. "I'm really sorry."

Aspen scratched Runa's chin. "It's okay, but you really do need to start paying attention."

Hazel sat down across from them, still unsure of the plan. "So did our flights get changed?"

"Hang on. I'll take care of it." She pulled her phone out and started texting rapidly.

"Why did your flights get changed?" Runa asked.

"Because we're going to California instead."

Runa gasped. "The ocean is in California. I'm coming with."

"No, you're not. We're looking for Rowan. We don't have time to watch you too. Besides, we're flying on an airplane." Hazel wasn't crazy about Runa. Plus this was the first possible lead they had, and she wasn't about to let a little dragon ruin it.

"Please. I can help."

"Airplane. You can't fly on an airplane." Runa didn't know how to take a hint.

"Oh yes I can." Then Runa disappeared out of the room.

"She realizes that you can see the ocean in Florida too, right?" Hazel asked Aspen.

Aspen shrugged and laughed. "You're probably not going to win this one. I bet she ends up on the flight with you."

Val entered the room with his hands in his pockets and his head down, followed by Runa. "Tell them I can help. Pleeeeeeaaaaaase." She landed on the table with a bag clutched in her claws.

"What's this?" Aspen asked.

"A cat carrier. No one looks too closely, and I can meow. Listen." She let out an awful screech that had them all covering their ears.

"Don't do that again," Hazel said and opened the cat carrier. She couldn't believe she was considering taking Runa with them.

"You know, she really could be helpful once we hit California," Val said. "She can fly and cover more ground than we can do on our own."

"Won't people be suspicious if they see her flying around?" He had a point though.

"River dragons will sometimes get that far north. If she changes so she's pure yellow, she can pass for one of them."

"So I can go?" Runa bounced up and down on the table.

"Calm down," said Aspen. "That entirely up to Hazel."

Hazel couldn't help but wonder if she was about to make a big mistake.

CHAPTER 17

"DO YOU WANT the window or the aisle?" Val asked. Hazel shrugged. "It's all the same to me." Truthfully Hazel was scared to death, but it had nothing to do with the plane. Though she was sure that would come soon. The last time she was on an airplane with Val, she'd had the kiss of her life, and as good as that was, she didn't want a replay because she wasn't sure she'd be able to walk away again.

"Why don't you take the window? I think I hogged it last time."

Hazel handed Runa to Val, shoved her backpack in the overhead, and slid into the seat. First class. Again.

The flight attendant stopped Val.

"Oh, is that a cat or dog?"

"Cat," Val said.

"I love kitties," she said and stuck her face close to the mesh lining at the front of the carrier.

Runa growled and the flight attendant jumped back, putting hand on her chest. The problem with Runa growling was that it was quite a bit louder than a normal cat. Not to mention that sometimes smoke came out.

Val quickly handed the carrier to Hazel.

"She doesn't like flying," he explained to the startled flight attendant.

"I guess not," she replied.

Hazel slid the carrier under the seat in front of her, and Runa grumbled something about it being too small.

"Be quiet," hissed Hazel. "It's a short flight. You'll be fine."

Runa answered by shoving her face against the mesh and glaring at her.

Hazel looked out the window and felt Val shift in the seat next to her. The plane pushed away from the gate, and Hazel's nerves got the better of her again. She gripped the edge of the seat and hoped Val hadn't noticed. She forgot all about Runa.

"Can I hold your hand again?"

Hazel didn't look at him, but she offered him her hand. He took it, and she felt her nerves calm. Once the plane was safely in the air, she let go and exhaled.

"Thank you," she said and looked at him. Big mistake. Why'd he have to be so beautiful?

"Anytime." He gave her a grin, and her stomach fluttered. "Have you ever been to Yosemite?" he asked her.

"Yeah, it's beautiful. Full of mountains and trees and waterfalls."

"Sounds like Yellowstone."

Hazel shrugged. "It's a different kind of beauty. Just like every beach is different even though they are all made of sand and water and setting suns."

"I'd like to go to the beach with you sometime."

Hazel flinched. "Maybe." They had a short flight. Only an hour, but he was trapped and couldn't escape. She leaned closer to him. "Can I ask you a question?"

"Of course."

"Why did a tattoo appear on my ankle with your name on it?"

He leaned back. "I don't know what you're talking about."

"You're lying. Why?"

He was so infuriating. She barely talked to him at all, and when she finally asked him a question he could answer, he clammed up.

"Did you talk to your sister?"

Hazel rolled her eyes. "Yep. She was a little vague."

"I think you should talk to her again."

"Why? The name on my ankle is Valentine, not Aspen."

"Because she can explain it better than I can."

Hazel was confused. "How does she know about it?"

"Ask her."

"I did. She said to ask you." Hazel hated being left in the dark. Both Val and Aspen were hiding what they really knew. They tried to play dumb, but Hazel saw right through them.

"Maybe none of us really understand what they mean."

"Then why didn't you just say that instead of being evasive."

"Because we have suspicions. But I don't want to scare you with suspicions."

Now they were getting somewhere. If Hazel kept him talking, she might actually get the answers she sought.

A humming noise came from in front of her. Hazel strained her ears. It was the wedding march. Who would be humming the wedding march? After a few seconds, she realized that it was coming from underneath the seat in front of her. Runa. Hazel kicked the carrier. Not hard, just enough to let Runa knew she was out of line. Runa responded with a loud, "Ow," and then a growl. Thankfully Hazel was pretty sure that only she and Val could hear it. Maybe the person whose seat she was under, but he didn't turn around or anything, so perhaps they got lucky.

Hazel crossed her arms. "Suspicions are better than nothing."

Val squeezed his eyes shut. "I don't know how to explain it."

"Do you have one too?"

"You mean a mark on my ankle?"

"Yeah."

He nodded. Hazel wondered what it looked like. Over that past few days, she'd grown to really like hers. It was beautiful.

"So tell me. Why do you think we have the marks?"

"I don't know. It just happens sometimes around the dragons. Aspen has a better understanding, but even she seems as lost as the rest of us."

Hazel was pretty sure he was lying. This mystery was huge, but with the search for Rowan, she couldn't give it too much thought, but as soon as they found him and brought him back home safely, she'd get to the bottom of this.

She leaned closer to him, figuring she'd give this one last shot. "If I kiss you again, will another one appear?"

Val blinked at her. Then he shook his head.

"Fine. Don't tell me." She'd given him every opportunity to explain. She'd even offered him the one thing she knew he'd wanted since they arrived in Montana. Then again, maybe he didn't. Maybe she'd just been thinking he wanted more, but he didn't, and here she was throwing herself at him like a fool.

She pulled out her phone, put on her headphones, and turned on the music. She looked out the window, and they didn't say another word to each other the rest of the flight.

But she did let him hold her hand as they landed.

CHAPTER 18

VAL WAS FRUSTRATED. He'd had her talking on the airplane, and then she went prickly because he wouldn't tell her about the mark. How could he? Every time he opened his mouth he was afraid he'd tell her too much. For a second he thought about telling her everything. But he couldn't risk her running. He needed her to really want to be with him first. Otherwise she could get scared, and he might never see her again.

At least that was what Aspen said.

And so far Aspen was usually right.

Val waited with Runa while Hazel rented the car. He felt so helpless as a human. He didn't know how to do things most of them took for granted. Like driving. When Hazel started talking to him again, he'd ask her to teach him.

She waved him over, and he followed her outside.

"Sid booked the car. I had no idea he loved me so much," she said with a grin.

"What do you mean?"

"Because we're driving that." She pointed to the car in front of them. It was a pretty blue.

"It's missing the top half," Val said.

"Yep. Convertible. Come on."

She tossed her backpack into the back and jumped into the driver's seat.

He put Runa's carrier on the backseat and eased himself down into the passenger side.

"Can I come out now?" Runa asked.

"We need to get out of the airport first. You still have to hide, but you won't have to ride in the carrier."

"I want to see the ocean."

"Runa, we came here to find my brother. If we have time after that, we'll take you to the ocean, but for now, we're heading inland. We've got a couple hours' drive. We'll stop at the gas station and get some snacks. I'll let you out then, but you may need to sit on the floor so no one sees you."

Something about the convertible changed Hazel. She was happy, excited. She chattered as they drove. Mostly about silly things. He was comfortable, and if he let himself forget he was supposed to be winning her over, he almost relaxed.

They drove up a winding mountain road, and the scenery started to change. The trees got taller and air cooler. Hazel handed the park ranger a card, and he waved her on in.

"We'll go to the main visitor center first, and then we'll fan out to the outer ones. Do you have the pictures?"

As soon as she put the car into park, he handed her a picture Aspen had taken of Rowan and Skye together. They looked like a happy couple. Hazel creased her eyebrows when she saw the picture.

"What's wrong?"

"I guess I've never seen Rowan so happy before. And Aspen was right. Skye's a knockout."

Val shrugged and held Hazel's gaze. "I've seen prettier."

She blushed, and he was pleased he got a reaction out of her. She focused her attention on Runa.

"You ready?"

"Yes. I'm so tired of hiding."

They took Runa's carrier out into the woods where no one could see them. They let her out, and she stretched out her wings. Val watched as she changed her body to a bright yellow.

"Can I pass for a river dragon?"

Val nodded.

Hazel crouched down. "I know you're excited to be somewhere new, but it's very important that you look for Rowan and Skye."

"I care about them too, you know." Runa flapped her wings.

Hazel stood. "Meet us back here when it gets dark."

She took off, and Hazel and Val headed back to the visitor center.

They asked the rangers and guests if they'd seen Skye and Rowan, but everyone shook their heads. After an hour, they made their way across the parking lot to the general store. The sun was dipping low in the sky, and Val knew they'd have to find a place to stay.

They spread out, and both took a couple of pictures. A few people remarked that they'd know if they'd seen Skye. But mostly they shrugged and said no.

"Let's get some food and a couple rooms at the lodge," Hazel said with a frown. "Then we'll need to go find Runa. It's getting late."

Hazel took Val's hand, and they wove through the crowded aisles. Val hoped his hand wouldn't sweat too much. A little girl ran in front of him, and as he dodged her, he ran into a rack of keychains and sent several scattering onto the floor. Hazel bent down to help him pick them up.

"All these people and not a single one has seen Skye or Rowan. Maybe our intel was bad."

Val shrugged. "Maybe. We'll keep asking. All we need is one person."

Hazel hung up the last keychain, which said "Mary" on it. Then grabbed his hand again.

"Come on, I'm hungry."

The store aisles gave way to a large tiled space with tables scattered about. Every single table was full of hoodie-wearing families and hikers. They joined the line of people waiting for food.

Hazel ordered a chicken sandwich and fries, and Val asked for the same.

"Will that be everything?" the man behind the counter asked.

Hazel looked back up at the menu. "Can I get a rotisserie chicken as well?"

"You hungry?" Val asked.

"No, but Runa will be."

"Good thinking."

As they were paying for the food, Hazel handed the picture to the cashier.

"This is my brother and his girlfriend. They were in Yosemite last week, and we lost contact with them. Have you seen them?"

The man studied the picture for a second.

"Yeah. I have. They were in here yesterday getting food. But the boy didn't have any glasses on. They looked a little rough around the edges. Like they'd been camping for a while."

Hazel's eyes lit up. "Did they give you any indication of where they might be staying?"

The man shook his head. "But they were definitely here."

"If you see them again, will you call me?" Hazel took a pad of Post-its out of her backpack and scrawled her number on it. Val admired her ability to think quickly. He still was so unsure of himself. In human form anyway.

"Sure thing," the man said with a nod.

They carried away their food. "Let's eat before we get a room. I don't want the food getting cold." They sat at a picnic table near the lodge and discussed possibilities as they ate.

"They're probably in a campground in the park. They wouldn't come all the way in here to get food if they were camping outside the park." Hazel studied the map. "We'll hit up all the campgrounds tomorrow and see if we can find them. We're close. I can feel it." She stared up at Val, and his heart beat faster. "Is Skye really in danger?"

Val nodded. "There's a list of seven people who could be killed. Two of them are already dead." Val hated to think that his dad was on that list as well. He'd just found him and didn't want his time to be cut short.

Hazel's shoulders drooped. "They probably wouldn't hesitate to kill Rowan either, would they?"

"No, they wouldn't." Val hated thinking about the possibilities of his own survival, let alone the danger all of his friends were in.

"What kind of a family do you belong to anyway?"

"A power hungry one. Let's go get a room, and then we'll fetch Runa."

"We've got time. I want to know more about your family."

"There's really not much to tell." Val wanted to tell Hazel everything. He really did. But she was just starting to open up to him. He didn't want to scare her away.

"You're being pretty vague."

"My family is protective of its secrets. I can't go telling just anyone."

Hazel harrumphed. "I'm not just anyone. I bet Aspen knows."

"Then ask Aspen," Val said and gathered up his tray. He walked away from her because he knew if he kept talking, he'd tell her too much. Hazel strode past him into the lodge without a backwards glance, thoroughly peeved. Val couldn't help but admire the view from behind. He wondered how pissed she'd be if she knew he was looking.

CHAPTER 19

"WHAT DO YOU mean there's only one room left?"
Hazel gaped at the man standing behind the front desk.
This was like a bad romance movie.

"Ma'am, it's a Saturday night. You're lucky it's January. If it were
June, there'd be no rooms left."

Hazel scratched her head. "At least tell me it has two beds."

The man grinned. "Yeah, it does. Here's your key."

Val waited in the lobby watching a family argue near the doors.
Sometimes he acted completely normal, but other times it was as if
he'd never been around humans at all. However, his kiss spoke of years
of experience. Hazel squeezed her eyes shut and opened them again.
She shouldn't think about that. Not when she was about to sleep five
feet from him.

She kicked his boot to get his attention. "Hey, we've got a room.
You ready?"

He shrugged and picked up his backpack. "That family over there, why do you think they're fighting?"

There was a mom and a dad, two teenagers, and one toddler. The mom looked about fifteen years younger than the dad.

"I'd guess the teenagers belong to the dad and the toddler is the love child. Chances are the teens hate their new stepmother, and dad is frustrated by their insolence. This exact scene is playing out all over the nation. Though I have friends who love their stepparents."

They walked back outside and into the darkening woods. Hazel hoped Runa would be there already. She didn't really relish the thought of waiting out here long.

"What's a stepparent?"

"You know, when parents get divorced and remarried. It's quite common."

They found the grove of trees where Runa flew off that morning. She wasn't there. Hazel settled on the ground and leaned up against a tree. Val sat across from her.

"What's divorce?" he asked, playing with a few pine needles on the ground.

"Divorce is where you get unmarried." Hazel was slightly uncomfortable. She couldn't believe he'd never even heard of divorce. It wasn't a happy topic to discuss.

Val creased his eyebrows. "Why?"

"Why what?"

"Why would someone get unmarried? I've never heard of such a thing."

"Lots of reasons. Mostly because they fall out of love. They grow apart and want a chance to love again." Hazel always figured if she got married, she'd end up divorced. Good thing she was never going to do such a thing.

"How do people fall out of love?"

Hazel snorted. "It happens. Trust me. I'm glad too, or I'd still be pining over Teddy."

"Maybe you never loved him in the first place."

"No, it hurt bad. If that wasn't love, I don't want to know what it feels like to fall in love and get crushed." Hazel studied him. "You're telling me you've never known anyone who's gotten married and then divorced?"

"No, but then again, my circle was small."

"Well, what happened if someone died? Would they get remarried then?"

"No, they'd live alone." Val looked up to the sky, but it was still Runa free.

"That sounds depressing."

"You're alone."

Hazel laughed. "No, I'm not. I'm not in an exclusive relationship, but I never lack for company."

Val frowned at her. "I hope someday you change your mind. There's something magical about so desperately wanting to be with someone that you never tire of their company. Something magical about having your souls connected in such a way that it's hard to see where you stop and they begin."

Hazel blinked for a second and crossed her arms. "You sound like you're speaking from experience."

He shook his head. "No, but I've seen it, and I won't settle for anything less."

Hazel didn't know how to respond, so she changed the subject. "Where do you think Runa is?"

Val shrugged. "Maybe she's holed up somewhere else. I say we wait another fifteen minutes or so and then go to bed. Even if she has to sleep out here, she'll be fine."

"That doesn't sound very nice. I wouldn't want to be stuck outside." Hazel was surprised she just defended Runa. What was happening to her?

Val stood and held out his hand for her. "She's a dragon. She's probably halfway to the ocean by now. But let's walk for a little bit and see if she just has the wrong spot."

They called her name as they stalked through the forest, but Runa didn't respond. After a half hour, they gave up and went into the lodge. Val didn't seem bothered by the fact that Runa was missing, but Hazel had a sinking feeling in her stomach. What if she was in trouble? In spite of Hazel's feelings for dragons, Runa had grown on her. She seemed almost human.

They quickly got ready for bed. Hazel lay awake for a long time that night, Val's words about love running over and over in her head. She'd thought she was in love with Teddy, but she never felt the same way about him that she felt about Val. Maybe Val was right. She didn't think she was missing out on anything, but now her heart ached for that kind of love he spoke of. She'd never wanted it before. What would it be like to feel like that about someone? Had she ever seen it before?

Sure. Her parents. They were united in every decision. They worked together, but they never tired of each other's company.

A light was streaming in through the crack in the curtains, and she could see Val's face. He was beautiful. There was no denying that. Every time she closed her eyes, she saw his face.

He seemed fascinated with her for some reason. She had no idea why. She was scared of falling for him though, because if she did, that would mean opening her heart up for shattering again. Maybe Val was different.

CHAPTER 20

VAL WOKE EARLY the next morning. Hazel sprawled out on her bed, her hair spread everywhere and her limbs all tangled in her blanket. The conversation they had last night bothered him. Her ideas of relationships and love were completely different from his. He knew she was to be his queen, but he didn't know how to convince her of that.

He took a shower, and when he got out, she was sitting up in bed.

"I'm going to shower real quick. Can you go check and see if Runa is sleeping in the woods?"

Val nodded. He didn't admit it to her last night, but Runa missing bothered him as well. Sure, she was a dragon, but he didn't think she'd just not show up when she was supposed to. She was a little ornery, but she listened when it counted.

He threw on a hoodie, hiked back to the woods, and called out for Runa. There was no response but his own voice. He searched the trees, hoping to spot anything bright yellow, but there was nothing. High up in a pine, a golden eagle watched him. He whistled and waved the eagle down. Sid had told him they would carry messages for them.

The eagle landed and bowed deeply.

Can I help you, Your Majesty?

Val froze for a second. He didn't know if he'd ever get used to being called that. "I'm missing a friend. She's a small river dragon. Can you put out the word that she's missing and I want her found."

Of course. When shall I report on what I've found?

"Meet me here tonight, right after sunset. If I'm not here, wait for me."

Val didn't waste any time getting back to the lodge. He knew Hazel wanted to find her brother as soon as possible. To his surprise, the light to the bathroom was still off, and the room was silent. He shut the door with a soft click and saw her still in bed, fast asleep.

He watched her, wondering what his life would be like if they were in a relationship. Just to be able to touch her whenever he wanted. He often had to hold back from brushing her arm or kissing her neck. He supposed part of that was the sealing, but maybe he was just in love. He was grateful winning her over fell under his duties as king, or he'd be terribly distracted.

He sat on the bed, and she didn't even stir. He tentatively placed his hand on her shoulder and gave her a light shake. Her eyes flew open, and she sat up, running right into him. He chuckled.

"You okay?" He scooted back a little bit to give her space.

"I didn't sleep well last night." She rubbed her eyes and looked around. "Where's Runa?"

"I don't know."

"Oh great, now we'll have to look for her too. We don't have time for this." She spoke with wild gestures, and her eyes revealed her panic.

"Hey," he said softly and grabbed her flailing hands. He pulled himself closer to her and looked her in the eyes. "Listen." Her breath came in rapid bursts, but she kept his eye. "I already thought of that. I enlisted the help of the eagles to search for Runa so we can focus on Rowan and Skye. They'll check in with me tonight."

Her breathing slowed just a little bit. "Eagles?"

"Yes. They help the dragons out quite a bit."

"Why don't we have the eagles looking for Skye and Rowan?"

She was so close to him. If he just leaned forward a few inches, he could kiss her again. But he didn't because that wouldn't be right. Not in this moment.

"Who do you think told us Skye was in Yosemite?"

Hazel leaned back. "For real?"

"Yeah."

Her panic had disappeared, and determination filled her features once again. She swung her legs out of bed.

"Then we need to get going. I'm going to shower, and then we'll grab some breakfast and check out the campgrounds. If we wait too long, they might be gone."

Val watched her dig through her bags and gather her clothes.

"Are you watching me?" she asked as she pulled out a red shirt and shorts.

He nodded. "Sorry. Can't help myself." A blush rose in his face.

She looked as if she wanted to say something, but then she left and locked herself in the bathroom.

Hazel leaned against the bathroom door and tried to still her shaking hands. What had Val done to her out there? She didn't have panic attacks very often, but occasionally they snuck up on her. The airplane was where they popped up most often, but sometimes when life overwhelmed her, she'd freak out. She'd felt it building out there, but he'd made it disappear.

She still could feel the anxiety in her chest, but this was for a very different reason. She put her clothes on the counter and looked at herself in the mirror for a few seconds. She didn't like the thoughts she was having. The ones where she wanted to kiss Val. Or touch him. Or simply relax around him.

She had a mission, and it had nothing to do with falling in love.

She stepped in the shower and hissed. The water was cold. She turned the tap until the water ran a comfortable temperature. To be honest, trying to deny her feelings for Val were more distracting than if she just gave in.

It was the reason she hadn't slept the night before. She tossed and turned, trying to put his face, his smell, his very presence out of her mind. It was incredibly difficult with him sleeping so close. Once, around two a.m., she very nearly crawled into bed with him, thinking she could just sleep if she curled up next to him. Thankfully she was aware enough to realize that would be a bad idea.

What would change if she allowed herself to give in? She wouldn't have to hold back. She could just be with him, and it would be far easier than trying to deny her feelings. A hell of a lot less distracting too. She knew how he felt about her, and he hadn't done anything but support her. She'd be able to concentrate on finding Rowan instead of worrying about if she was doing the wrong thing with Val.

As she stepped out of the shower, a weight lifted off her shoulders. This was one less thing she would have to worry about. She'd chill around Val, and if that led to love and kisses, then she'd let it. She felt a little stupid that she'd been fighting against this, since it made everything more difficult. And she needed things to be easy now.

Hazel smelled like lavender. She pulled the map out of her bag and sat next to him on the bed. Her legs touched his. She seemed more relaxed. More open.

She unfolded the map and set it across both of their laps. "There are only four campgrounds open this time of year, but they could be backcountry camping. They'd need a permit for that though, so we can check with the log. I say we go to the campgrounds first."

"Okay, lead the way."

Val followed her out. For Hazel's sake he hoped they found them. Hell, for his sake. They needed a win. He was nervous that they lost Runa. Personally, he hoped she'd just found something interesting and got distracted. Also he didn't want to be the one who told Sid that he lost her.

They talked to anybody they saw, but no one had seen either Rowan or Skye at the campgrounds.

Hazel leaned against the car at Wawona Campground and blew her bangs out of her face. "This sucks. Let's go back to the visitor center and ask to look at their permit logs."

"Do you really think they're going to let you do that?"

Hazel nodded. "I took one of my mom's IDs. I look just like her, so they'll let me study the log."

"Sneaky." Val was a little surprised she'd thought of it. He wondered what other tricks she had up her sleeve.

She shrugged. "I thought we might need it."

It took them an hour to drive back to the visitor center. Val could see the stress building around Hazel's eyes again. The ranger handed Hazel the logbook. "There's a couple of pages. It shouldn't take you too long to find."

"We're going back about a week."

"Good luck."

Hazel studied the names carefully. Val read over her shoulder, but he didn't see anything that looked like Skye or Rowan.

Hazel slammed the book shut. "This is impossible."

"Maybe they are camping without a permit."

"Rowan knows better."

"But if he doesn't want to be found, he might risk it."

"True."

"Why don't we grab lunch from the general store and hike a couple of trails. Flash those pictures around some more." Val just wanted to keep moving. She seemed more at ease when they were out doing something.

They hiked most of the day and barely even saw other people. The sun was hanging low in the sky when they reached a small lake.

"Why don't we eat here before we head back down," Val suggested.

She nodded, but her face betrayed her sadness.

"Hey, what's wrong?" he asked.

"What if he's gone? What if we don't find him?"

Val put his hand on her back. "Don't think like that. We'll find him."

She leaned into him. Surprised, he pulled her close. She buried her face in his chest and snaked her arms around his back. He held her against him. He had no idea what to say. He'd never tried to comfort a girl before.

Too soon, she pulled away. "Thanks." She gave him a sheepish grin and headed down to the lake. He followed her, optimistic for the first time in a long time. Her hips swung as she walked, and she stretched as she reached the shore, raising her arms above her head. He wanted to reach out and touch the strip of skin that showed between her shirt and shorts.

The ground behind him shook, and he spun. A bright orange canyon dragon stood menacingly over them. Hazel screamed. Val grabbed her hand and pulled her close to him.

Since when does a king fall for a weak human girl like that? I thought queens were supposed to be strong.

Leave her out of this. What do you want?

How could he get Hazel out of there without the canyon dragon noticing? He wasn't sure what the canyon dragon wanted, but it wasn't good.

The dragon snorted, and orange smoke poofed out of its nose. *Oh, you're right. Nothing good. A war is starting, or didn't you know that? Imagine how pleased the witch will be when I tell her I killed the new king and his queen.*

Val had forgotten that canyon dragons could read thoughts. He'd never met one before. He paused for a second. If he put Hazel out of his thoughts all together, then maybe the dragon would focus on him and leave her alone. If she was smart, she'd run. And Hazel was smart.

Val shoved her away from him and prepared to change. Time slowed to a near stop as the canyon dragon swept her with his wing. Her body flew through the air, limbs flailing, and she hit the ground with a sickening thud, her head cracking on a rock. Then time sped up, and Val waited for her to make a move. Even a twitch. Nothing. The canyon dragon would pay for this with his life. Val changed into a dragon and let out a jet of flames in frustration. He remembered what his father taught him and took flight, heading straight for the canyon dragon's eyes.

But the dragon lifted off the ground, and Val had to climb higher, looking for another opening to the eyes. He found it and zeroed in on the head. But the dragon moved at the last minute and slashed at Val's neck, leaving a wide gash.

Your father didn't teach you how to fight against us. I know your every move before you even make it. Go ahead, think of what you want to do next.

Val circled him, completely lost. He wished there was an easy opening. Canyon dragons had very slender necks. It wouldn't be that hard to just bite off his head.

Except you'll never get that opening. Good thoughts on the eyes though. That would make things more difficult. I'll remember that the next time I'm in a fight.

Val still wasn't sure how he was going to win this. He was glad the canyon dragon hadn't made any moves yet either. He was probably a little intimidated as fire dragons were quite a bit larger than they were.

Nah, I'm just playing with you.

A flash of yellow appeared above. Runa landed on the canyon dragon's head before he could even register that she was there. The canyon roared as Runa clawed out his eyes. Val saw his opening and took it, banking on the dragon being way too distracted to hear his thoughts. His jaws clamped down on the soft flesh, and blood burst everywhere as the dragon's head and his body went in two different directions. Runa let go of this head, and it fell to the ground.

"That was disgusting," Runa exclaimed.

It was necessary. Thank you for your help. He turned and flew down to Hazel and changed into his human form. He put his head against her chest and felt it rise and fall. Then he let out a breath of relief.

"She's alive."

Runa landed next to him. "We should probably get her to a doctor. I'd say take her to the woodlands, but with the canyon dragons floating around, most of the woodland dragons are hiding. It would take too long to find one."

Val looked at Hazel, unsure of how to proceed. What if she woke up on the flight? He wasn't sure what he would tell her, but it was time for her to know the truth. He changed back into his dragon form and gently picked her up with his claws.

CHAPTER 21

AZEL'S HEAD HURT. A lot. But that wasn't what was bothering her. It was the wind. Her hair was whipping across her face. She cracked her eyelids open and gasped. She was hundreds of feet up in the air. What was she doing in the air? She swiveled her head around, but that made her dizzy. She closed her eyes again and opened them. Above her she could see a massive black dragon head with long fangs visible just below his chin. Claws held her tight. She couldn't even begin to comprehend what was happening. A stab of pain pierced through her head, and she lost consciousness.

Hazel blinked her eyes open. A soft light filtered in through a window. She sat up. Her head still hurt, and her arms were stiff.

"Oh good, you're awake."

Hazel grinned. "Runa, when did you get back?"

"I had to save you from that canyon dragon. How are you feeling?"

"What time is it?"

"Don't know. Mid-morning maybe. Val left you some food."

Hazel's stomach growled. "How long was I unconscious?"

"You mean asleep?"

"Yeah."

"Well, the doctors checked you out last night and said you were fine. You woke up for a little while but seemed really confused."

"I don't remember that."

"You were asking for your mom and dad. You didn't know Val at all. The doctors said you were probably suffering from short term amnesia."

"Why am I not in a hospital?"

"Dunno. Val said you would be better off here."

"Where is he anyway?"

"Out searching. He said you wouldn't want the search to stop just because you were hurt. He'll check back in a couple of hours."

Holy cow. If she wasn't in love before, she sure was now. Most men wouldn't have left her side, but he went after the more important thing. She was an idiot for trying to hold him at bay.

Hazel carefully got out of bed. "He's right." Her legs were a little shaky as she walked over to the table. She picked up a banana and took a bite. She'd need food if she was going to find her brother.

"Where's my phone?"

"By the television. Been buzzing all morning. Driving me crazy."

Hazel picked it up. There were several missed calls. All from the same number. She immediately dialed it back.

"Hello," said a deep voice.

"This is Hazel. You've been trying to reach me."

"Oh, yeah, I'm a clerk at the general store in Yosemite. You gave me your number and told me to call you if I saw the blonde woman and her boyfriend."

Hazel straightened. "And?"

"They were here this morning. I tried to stall them, but they've already left."

Dammit. "Did they say anything about where they were going?"

"Not to me, but I eavesdropped on their conversation. They kept talking about going to a cave on the coast. But I don't know which one."

"Did you ask?"

The man chuckled. "I did. They said it wasn't a public one, and then they left. I'm sorry."

Hazel sighed. "Thank you. I appreciate your help." Hazel hung up the phone and tried to figure out how much time had passed since they left Montana.

"Runa, what day is it?"

"Monday."

Her mom was going to kill her. But she couldn't go home. Not now. She fired off a quick message to Aspen.

Got a lead. Can't go home. Make sure you're there for the funeral, or mom's going to kill us both.

Hazel went outside and saw Val walking between cars. She waved him over.

"Any luck?" she asked him.

"No. How are you feeling?" He brushed her hair out of her face, and her insides buzzed.

Hazel waved her phone. "I just got a call from a store clerk who saw Skye and Rowan. They're headed to a cave on the coast."

Val rubbed his hand along his face. "They could be going anywhere."

Hazel shrugged. "Maybe. But there is really only one road to the coast. We can show their pictures around at convenience stores and see if people have seen them."

Val sighed. He opened his mouth and closed it again. Then he shook his head. "Okay, let's go check out those convenience stores."

Runa, who was crammed in Hazel's backpack, let out a "yay."

"What are you so excited about?" Hazel asked.

"I finally get to see the ocean."

"Come on, just for thirty minutes. Please," Runa whined.

"We aren't stopping for you to play in the water."

"I've been trapped on the floor for hours while you two keep going inside stores. I'll be able to actually look. Didn't you say they were looking for a cave?"

"Yes. But the last time we let you out, you disappeared for a day, and you still won't tell us where you were."

Runa harrumphed.

They'd been searching for several hours, stopping the car and flashing the picture around gas stations and convenience stores. No one had seen them. Hazel was starting to get discouraged.

Val had his arm slung on the back of her seat, and she enjoyed having him close.

"Maybe Runa's right. There's a beach down there. Let's get some food and go sit on the beach and eat. It's basically deserted. Runa can go play in the water, and then she can search the cliffs over there. It's faster if she flies by them and looks instead of having to hike down and search them."

Hazel hesitated, then agreed. She didn't know what else they'd do right now anyway. She was lost as to what to do next.

She and Val sat in the sand a little ways up the beach. Runa dive bombed into the water as soon as she took off. She came up crowing. Hazel scooted closer to Val. She wanted him to put his arm around her or hold her hand or something. But he was keeping his distance.

"I'm not going home until I find them," she finally said.

"I know. I have no intention of leaving your side." A splash out in the water drew his eyes away from Hazel. Runa had belly flopped in the water. "You have to admit having Runa around is useful."

"Yeah. She's kind of annoying though, isn't she?"

As if on cue, she landed right in front of them, spraying sand everywhere.

"Not going home, ever. I want to be a beach dragon."

"Well, for now, you're in luck. We'll be staying near the water until we find Rowan or discover he went somewhere else. You ready to go search those cliffs and see what's in the caves?"

Runa nodded her now blue head and flew off to the cliffs.

As soon as she was out of sight, Hazel saw movement out of the corner of her eye. A surfer had come down to the beach, and he took the waves.

"Do you miss it?" Val asked.

"Of course. But the waves here are nothing like the ones in Hawaii. That poor guy has no idea what he's missing."

Val didn't have a clue what he was doing. He was here with a beautiful girl on the beach. They had some time before Runa returned, and even though he really wanted to kiss her, he didn't think it would be appropriate.

Val watched Hazel with interest. She was looking a little too appreciatively at the surfer, who was now far out in the water.

"Holy hell, what is that?" Hazel asked.

Val snapped his eyes back to the water. A large flying mass was heading straight for the surfer. Val jumped up.

It was a gold dragon. He knew that dragon. He was flying low and fast, and Val realized what he was about to do seconds before Hazel did. They had to get out of there before they were seen, but Hazel was running for the water waving her hands. Val grabbed her and put a hand over her mouth before she screamed. She struggled against him as they both watched the gold dragon snap the surfer up whole.

Val whispered in Hazel's ear. "We have to stay silent. We don't want him to see us, or we'll be the next to die."

She nodded against his shoulder, and he moved his hand off of her mouth. The gold dragon flew farther out to sea. Val waited until they couldn't see him at all before he spoke.

"Let's go," he said to Hazel, grabbing her hand and pulling her back up the beach.

"I could've warned him," Hazel said, jerking her hand out of his.

"No, you couldn't have. You would've been too late. If you had shouted at him, the only thing that would've happened is we would both be dead too. We need to go."

Hazel stomped her foot and glared at him, then crossed her arms and stalked back toward the car.

Val pulled his phone out and dialed Sid as he walked.

He and Hazel were the only witnesses. He needed to keep it that way. If the media thought the dragon was out here as well, there would be a bloodbath.

The phone went straight to voicemail. Dammit.

He caught up with Hazel as she started up the stairs.

"We need to get back to Montana."

"No, we need to find Rowan."

"We'll come back. I promise. But we have to go talk to Sid. His phone went to voicemail. That was the human killer, and now I know who he is. This ends now." Val couldn't quite believe what he just saw. He trusted that dragon, learned from him. His insides churned as he thought of what this would mean for Sid.

"What do you mean you know who he is?"

"Did Aspen explain that we know the dragons very well?"

"Yeah, she has a black dragon that she likes a lot."

Val didn't know how to explain without spilling the beans. "Okay, listen, that gold dragon. The one that just ate the surfer. He's the dragon that Sid is closest to. It's his best friend. I know him quite well too. This is no longer just some random dragon eating people. This is personal. We have to go back and tell Sid. Then, when everything is taken care of, we'll come back and search for Rowan. For now, we know he's alive and safe. He's with Skye."

"But you said she was in danger."

"She is. But so are all the rest of us. She's managed to avoid detection so far. Rowan might be safer with her than you are with me. Come on."

Runa landed on the ground next to the car. "Are we leaving already?"

Val nodded.

"Why?"

"I know who the human killer is."

"Who?" Runa cocked her head. Val knew he had to be careful how he phrased this. He hoped Runa would be smart enough to not say anything that would give them away.

"It's Prometheus."

CHAPTER 22

THE NEXT COUPLE of hours were a frenzy of getting ready and checking into the airport. Val didn't know how he was going to tell Sid. He hadn't known Theo long, but he was Sid's best friend. Treachery like that could break even the strongest of individuals.

As the plane pushed away from the gate, Hazel turned to him.

"You'll hold my hand again, right?"

Val smiled at her. "You know you don't even have to ask."

"You seem a little distant, so I wasn't sure."

"Sorry, I'm still not quite sure how to behave around you. I don't want to be too forward."

She took a deep breath and acted like she was going to say something, but then the plane shuddered, and she gripped his hand. She didn't say anything as the plane took off, but she took deep breaths.

Her eyes were closed. As the plane leveled off, she relaxed her hand but didn't let go.

She smiled at him. "I'm not sure I can fly anywhere anymore without you."

"I'm not complaining."

"We should definitely make sure we're together on the flight back to Hawaii."

He nodded, but he wasn't sure he would be going back to Hawaii. He wasn't sure if she would either.

Hazel didn't let go of his hand until the flight attendant brought them drinks and a snack. She chattered on for most of the flight. When the fasten seatbelt sign flashed back on, she gripped his hand again.

"Almost there."

Hazel nodded.

"Is there anything I can do to help you relax?"

She opened her eyes and looked at him. "Yes."

"What's that?" he asked, leaning closer.

Her face flushed. "Kiss me again."

She didn't have to ask him twice, but at the last second he stopped. Her face was inches from his. He watched her brilliant green eyes as they blinked, and ran his thumb along her jaw. She shivered.

"You need to promise me something."

"What?" she whispered.

"Promise me that you won't tell me to get lost after this is over. If I kiss you, we're in this for the long haul. I want to be yours and you to be mine. I don't want to share you with anyone."

She backed away a fraction of an inch and stared deep into his eyes. He was terrified she'd say no.

"Promise," she finally said.

His lips met hers, and she returned the kiss eagerly. She let go of his hand and wrapped her arms around his neck, pulling her close to him. He'd never felt so alive in his life.

A voice in the seat across the aisle from them yelled out. "This isn't an effing hotel room."

Hazel pulled away and giggled. She didn't even acknowledge the man who shouted. Instead, she kept her gaze locked on Val's as the plane touched down.

"I think kissing is a better distractor than hand holding," Hazel said.

"We should definitely do more of it then."

"Of course."

CHAPTER 23

H AZEL DROPPED Val off at Sid's house.

"Aspen sent me a message telling me she was home. I'm going to go say hi to my parents, and then we'll come back."

Val nodded and gave her a quick kiss. Truthfully, he was glad. He didn't want the fact that he was a dragon to come out in the middle of his conversation with Sid. He wanted to support Sid, and he couldn't do that if he was worried about what Hazel thought.

He found Sid was in the theater room watching the news.

A blonde newscaster stood bundled up with snow blowing all around her. "This is the latest in a string of deaths by a golden dragon. All national parks around the nation are being shut down. Government officials aren't saying anything except that they are taking steps to remedy the problem and have assured the public that no one else will die. That hasn't stopped protesters from all over the U.S. calling for the death of the dragons."

Sid muted the television and hung his head.

"Where is it?" Val asked.

"Alaska."

"Well, he makes good time then. Because he snatched a surfer up this afternoon."

Sid stood. "What the hell?"

Val waved him over. "You need to sit down. I know who he is."

Sid clenched his fists. "I will not sit down. Tell me. Who is it?"

Val took a step back. He didn't want to be in hitting range when Sid found out.

"Sid, I saw him. It's Theo."

Sid's face went ashen. He picked up a vase on the table next to the couch and threw it across the room. It shattered, sending shards everywhere. Then he clutched at his hair and sank down on the couch with his head hung.

"I've been so blind. Of course it's Theo. Who else was in both Hawaii and Alaska?"

Val sat next to Sid and put a hand on his shoulder.

"Look, I know this is a lot for you to process. But we need to catch him."

Sid sat up straighter, and his lips formed a tight line. "You know, this means he killed my father as well." Sid stood and paced. He opened and closed his fists. His breath came in rapid bursts. Val couldn't even begin to comprehend how he felt.

Pearl came into the room. "We've got to go to DC. The president is summoning you."

Sid shook his head. "Get her on the phone. I don't have time to go to DC. We know who it is. This ends as soon as we can find him. Fortunately, we have the advantage that he doesn't know we know who he is."

"Is it Kingston?" Pearl, asked with her eyes bugged. "He's been spending a lot of time up north."

Sid shook his head and let out hollow chuckle. "No. It's Theo."

Pearl gasped. "No. How?"

Val decided to answer for Sid. "He was in Hawaii when they had their deaths. Alaska too. Plus I saw him get a surfer in California a few hours ago."

Pearl put her arms around Sid. "Oh, Sid, I'm so sorry."

"It's time we finish this. I'd like to involve the National Guard around Yellowstone. If it looks like we are asking for their help, they might hold off doing something dumb, like nuking our nests. Pearl, get the damned president on the phone."

Sid and Pearl escaped into the office, and not long after, Val went into the kitchen with Runa. Hazel and Aspen were just coming through the back door.

Runa bobbed up and down on the table. "We found the human killer," she chirped.

Aspen sat down in front of her. "What? How'd you do that?"

"Saw him."

"Who is it?"

"Prometheus."

All the color drained out of Aspen's face. Her eyes flicked to Hazel. She kept her voice even, but her hands were shaking. "Really? Where's Sid?"

"On the phone with the president."

Sid came back into the room and froze when he saw the girls. "Hey. We're all meeting at the Theodore-Roosevelt Visitor Center at seven. Aspen, can I talk to you?"

"Sure."

She followed him out of the room, and Val reached for Hazel. She gave him a small smile.

"How are your parents?"

"As well as they could be. Aspen won't let me tell them anything about Rowan. I would love to head back to California and continue the search."

"We can't. We need to take care of the human killer. I have to stay here and help Sid. But as soon as he's dead, I'll go back to California with you."

Hazel creased her eyebrows. "What do you have to do?"

Val sighed. He needed to come clean sooner or later. Just as he got ready to speak, Runa stuck her snout in Hazel's face. "How come you don't like dragons?"

"Have you not seen the deaths that have occurred in the last few months?"

"But that's just one dragon."

"It doesn't matter. We can't control them. They pose a threat to us all. This was bound to happen sooner or later. You'll probably be able to take care of this one, but what happens when another dragon starts eating people?"

"Then we fix it, just like now."

"But how many people die in the meantime? They're just a nuisance."

"Are you calling me a nuisance?"

Hazel shrugged. "You're tiny. You pose no threat."

"I could bite your nose off." Runa bared her teeth and snapped her jaw once.

"But you won't. Runa, go make sure Aspen and Sid are okay," Val interjected. He wasn't about to try to break up a fight between Hazel and Runa. He'd never tell Hazel, but if it came down to it, Runa would win.

Runa rounded on him. "I don't like her. Can you find another girlfriend?" She spread her bright yellow wings and flew out of the kitchen, whacking Hazel on the head on her way.

"Here I thought I was growing on her. She's got nerve," Hazel said with a nervous laugh. Maybe Hazel did recognize that Runa would best her if given the chance.

Val took her hand. "You know, dragons are a part of my life. If we are going to be together, you'll need to get over your prejudices."

"Prejudices? They're animals. And I wasn't lying about them being a nuisance. Just like snakes, rats, or moles. Life would be easier without them around." She rubbed her forehead. "Can we talk about something else? I don't want to fight."

Val nodded, knowing they would have to deal with this sooner or later.

CHAPTER 24

VAL STOOD NEXT to Sid in the crowded visitor center. They were up on a small stage that was normally used for ranger talks. Val doubted when they built it, they ever imagined it being used to coordinate a dragon killing. National Guard members filled the room with a handful of civilians. Aspen was in the back with her parents and Hazel. Val smiled at Hazel, and she winked at him.

Sid commanded the crowd. Val could see why he was king. What he couldn't understand was his own transformation. He was never good at leading anything.

The crowd hushed as Sid began.

"We have identified the human killer. He will be arriving this evening. A handful of our dragons will meet him. We will make sure that no other golden dragons are around so that you will know exactly who he is. We will allow you to come with us under only one circumstance."

A man standing in the front glared at Sid. "What's that?"

"We want to ensure you will not intervene. Your purpose is to witness. That's all."

The man crossed his arms. "How many dragons are we talking?"

"Two black, two silver, and a red."

"That's not very many. Are you sure they can handle the gold dragon? We can help."

"If we bring in too many, he'll get suspicious and leave. We don't need help, but we do need you to see the destruction of the human killer so the public is appeased."

The man looked at the men on either side of him. "Sure. We can witness."

Sid dropped down next to him. He towered over the tiny man. "I want you to understand something. If you try anything, you will have a war on your hands. And the dragons will win."

"Do you doubt my word?"

"You give it rather carelessly."

"We won't hurt the dragons."

Sid backed up. "Okay, now that we have that out of the way. We've chosen a location surrounded by trees so you can effectively hide. Whoever is in charge of commanding the troops will have Aspen with him. She can communicate with the dragons."

Titters broke out across the room, and the defiant man spoke again. "How?"

Aspen stepped forward. "Dragons communicate telepathically. Last year I befriended one of the black dragons."

The man nodded to the young man standing next to him. "Paul will be leading the troops. You can coordinate with him. Hopefully tomorrow this will all be behind us, and I can go home to my wife."

Val caught Hazel's eye, and she had a frown on her face. He knew she wasn't crazy about dragons. He just hoped that as she learned more, she wouldn't run. Because he liked having her by his side, and he wasn't sure he'd be able to take it if she changed her mind.

CHAPTER 25

HAZEL DIDN'T KNOW what she was doing, sitting at the table in a conference room with Sid, Val, Aspen, Paul, and a few others she didn't know. She had absolutely nothing to contribute, but Val pulled her in anyway and held her hand in his lap. Paul glared at them, but she didn't care. Instead of worrying about the boys, she leaned over to Aspen.

"So how do you talk to dragons?"

Aspen shrugged. "With my mind. It's not a big deal."

"It is a big deal. Do they talk like us, or is it more rudimentary?" Hazel felt like she was on the cusp of understanding something big, but she couldn't put her finger on what. The dragons were key to whatever secrets Aspen and Val were keeping.

Aspen let out a laugh. "They are just as, if not more, intelligent than us. Obsidian, the black dragon, is my best friend."

Hazel scratched her head. "How are Val and Sid connected? Because I think the story about them being cousins is a lie."

"Not my secret to share, Sis."

Hazel looked sidelong at Val. They were together, and she cared for him a great deal, but she still didn't know him all that well. She wished she knew if it would be possible to push him into telling her or if he would just flee.

Sid stood and talked about logistics. Hazel didn't understand most of it, but her ears caught that Aspen and Paul would be hiding in the trees with a good view of where the fight was go to down. After Sid dismissed everyone, Hazel hung back. She was worried Val would notice, but he left the room deep in conversation with Sid. She caught Paul's arm.

He raised his eyebrows at her. "You and that dragon prick, huh?"

"Dragon prick?"

"That guy is on their side."

Hazel shrugged. "He's a nice guy. But yeah, we're together." Paul wouldn't like it, but she didn't really care what Paul thought.

Paul pulled her close. "That's never stopped you before."

She wiggled out of his embrace. "This is different. That's not why I wanted to talk to you." She hoped he'd cooperate, even without the promise of a kiss.

He rolled his eyes. "What do you want?"

"I want to go with you and Aspen tonight."

Paul crossed his arms and shook his head. "That is no place for civilians."

"Aspen's going." Why did everyone act like she was helpless?

"Aspen's not a civilian."

"Like hell she's not. She's my sister. I'm going with."

"Why? You've never cared much what happens to dragons."

"Because Aspen and the others are keeping something from me. Something that has to do with dragons. The more I get involved with things, the better chance I have at discovering it." Besides, she wanted to keep an eye on Aspen.

"Well, I'm not going to invite you along, but if you show up with Aspen, I won't turn you away."

Hazel nodded, determined to find a way to tag along with Aspen.

Out in the lobby, people were milling about, and all conversations buzzed of dragons. Val wrapped an arm around her waist and pulled her close. Hazel leaned into him and closed her eyes, wishing that all their problems would just go away.

"Hey, we've got a few hours before the action starts. You want to come back to the house with me?"

She planted a light kiss on his lips and frowned.

"I'd love to, but I've got business to take care of with Aspen. Tomorrow, this is all going to be over. Let's meet up tonight, and we'll stay in all day watching movies and gorging on pizza. How's that sound?"

He leaned down. "I'd like to do that now."

She pulled out of his arms. If she wasn't careful, she'd forget all about Aspen. "Me too, but surely you have a role to play in tonight's activities."

"I do."

"Where will you be when all this goes down?"

"Secret. But I'll explain everything tomorrow. If you're going to be a part of my life, you deserve to know everything."

Hazel's heart raced. Maybe she wouldn't have to go with Aspen at all if Val would just tell her. She grabbed his hand. "I'll go with you now, if you tell me this afternoon."

Sid approached from the side and clapped Val on the shoulder. "We need to get Damien and Athena, you coming?"

Val nodded and kissed Hazel on the tip of her nose. "Tonight. Promise. When everything is over."

She couldn't help but feel disappointed, but she left Val and Sid and went in search of Aspen, who was outside arguing with Paul.

"There will be no need for weapons. We're just watching."

Paul laughed in her face. "What is the point of us coming if we don't have weapons?"

"How many troops are you bringing with?"

"A hundred."

"You need to promise me you won't use them unless the dragons fail to take care of the human killer."

"I can't promise anything, sweetheart."

Aspen clenched her fists and took a deep breath. "Fine," she said and spun on her heel and stomped away.

"What time do you want to meet?" Paul called after her.

"Five. Here." She paused just long enough to answer and then continued her race for the door. Hazel ran after her.

She caught up with her seconds later. "Hey, you okay?" Hazel asked.

Aspen shook her head. "Something feels wrong about this. I need to find Sid."

"He and Val just went to get Athena and Damien. Are they dragons?"

Aspen nodded. "That means I won't be able talk to him. Let's go back to Sid's. I can see if Runa will help me. She may be able to get word to them."

Hazel hopped in the passenger seat. Once Aspen was on the road, Hazel brought up her own plans.

"Can I come with this evening?"

"To the dragon beheading?"

"Beheading?"

"Yeah, that's how they kill each other."

Hazel's insides squirmed. She didn't like blood and gore. "How do you know?"

"I saw it last year. Twice."

"That must be pretty gruesome." Hazel grimaced at the thought of dragons killing one another. The thought of the blood that must come out when they get beheaded was more than she could stomach.

"It is. Why do you want to come?"

"I just want to stay in the loop. Can I come?" She was so close to answers.

"I don't see why not. I didn't think you had a thing for dragons."

"I don't. But Val is wrapped up in all of this. I don't know how, but if it's part of his world, then it's part of mine."

"How on earth did you go from being a no commitment chick to this?" Aspen asked with a chuckle.

Hazel shrugged. Something about being with Val was different. He had a hold of her heart in a way that she didn't understand.

Back at the house, they found Runa and another bright yellow dragon in the kitchen.

"Runa, I need you to go out on a job for me," said Aspen.

Runa bounced up and down. "Yay, a job. What do I get to do?"

"I need you to find Sid and tell him the troops will all be bringing massive guns to the rendezvous. Something feels very wrong about this."

The other dragon snapped her head up. "She can't go. Someone out there wants her dead. She's just a baby." Hazel still wasn't used to dragons speaking, and it was weird seeing an animal talk like that.

Runa nudged the other dragon's neck. "Mama, you can't talk to Aspen like that. You know who she is." So that was her mom. Hazel wondered if even she could keep Runa in line.

"Forgive me. But you understand, I'm sure. Would it be okay if I went instead?"

Hazel raised her eyebrows. Why were these dragons talking about Aspen as if she was to be revered?

Aspen exhaled. "Do you know where Damien's cave is?"

The yellow dragon nodded. "Runa and I had to visit him this morning."

"Go. Quickly. They have to be warned."

Aspen sunk down in the chair. Runa rubbed against her forehead like a cat. "It's not fair that I didn't get to go."

"I'm not about to argue with your mom."

Runa snorted.

Hazel sat down slowly in the chair next to her. "What did Runa mean by her mom not being able to talk to you like that?"

Runa's eyes widened. "You mean you don't know?"

Aspen reached over and clamped Runa's mouth shut. "I'm pretty tight with the dragon king. That's not something most people can say. Runa's mom is afraid I'm going to blab to him."

Runa glared at Aspen, and Aspen let go of her mouth. "You people and your secrets. She's going to find out eventually. You might as well tell her."

Aspen shook her head. "Nope. I'm not going to be the one who spills the beans."

"You two are infuriating. What the hell are you talking about?" Hazel crossed her arms and gave both of them a death stare. She was sick of being treated like an outsider.

Aspen's eyes flashed to Hazel. "Sorry. I can't. You should ask Val. He needs to be the one to tell you everything."

"But Runa made it seem like it involves you."

Aspen snorted. "It absolutely involves me, but Val can tell you. I can't tell you my part without revealing his."

Hazel and Aspen crawled up into Paul's Humvee. Twenty or more were surrounding the visitor center. Hazel was a little nervous about the whole thing. She knew she was about to witness something awful. Not to mention that there were a million things that could go wrong.

"Can I see this gun you're bringing?"

Paul smirked at her. "No. Let's go."

"What if I refuse? The dragons can take care of themselves."

Paul laughed. "You won't. In order to appease the public, you have to prove this happened. You need us as witnesses."

Aspen crossed her arms and looked out the window. "I hate that you're right."

"Where to?"

"Follow the Grand Loop Road for about two miles. There'll be a turn off."

It was cold as Hazel settled in on the ground next to the tree. She was surprised at what a good view they had of the clearing. They were about twenty feet into the tree line. The troops all spread out so they were surrounding the entire clearing. Aspen had a pair of binoculars trained on the trees across the way.

"Hey, Paul," she said. "Let's say, hypothetically you decide to shoot one. Which you shouldn't do. Sid said he'd take care of the problem. We should trust him. But, pretend with me for a moment. What happens if you try to shoot one of those dragons and miss? It will probably hit someone on the other side of the circle."

Paul smirked at Aspen. "We won't miss."

"You can't shoot one of them."

"They're just dragons."

Aspen spun on him, her eyes blazing. Hazel agreed with Paul, but she would never say something like that.

"Do you have any idea what you are talking about? I value their lives more than my own. If you shoot one, I'll kill you, and I am not joking."

"Are you threatening me?"

"Yeah, I am." Aspen got right into his face. Hazel pulled her away. She didn't need Aspen punching him and starting the night off with a bang.

"Paul, she's passionate about the dragons. Give her a break. And, Aspen, don't threaten Paul." They didn't have time from drama. The dragons would be arriving any minute now.

"I don't plan on killing any of them except the human killer. And neither will anyone else. We have our orders."

"But if you miss," Aspen began, but Paul cut her off.

"We're highly trained. We won't miss."

Hazel picked up Aspen's discarded binoculars and looked to the sky. A mass was descending on the clearing.

"Aspen, check it out." She handed her the binoculars.

Aspen looked out into the clearing and a massive grin formed on her face. Paul brought out his own binoculars.

"Dammit. I thought he said there would only be a few of them."

Aspen held out a finger. "Obsidian said this was the only way to get Prometheus here without rousing suspicion. He called a meeting with all the royal dragons."

The ground shook as over a thousand dragons landed at once.

"Which one is Prometheus?" Paul asked.

Aspen shrugged. "Why would I tell you that?"

"Because I deserve to know."

"No, not really, you don't. You'll know who he is when he dies."

CHAPTER 26

VAL WAS NERVOUS because he'd didn't relish the thought of killing another. Sid said he'd do it, but Val had to be prepared for a fight if Sid failed in some way. This was the dragon that not only slaughtered dozens of humans, but also killed at least three dragons. Who knew what he was capable of?

Good thinking on calling all the royal dragons, Val said.

Stupid humans bringing massive guns. What were they thinking? I'm not looking forward to this.

I know.

Surrounding them was every royal dragon in Yellowstone, save a few they couldn't contact. None of them knew the nature of the meeting, but they came anyway. Sid said after this, the whole world would know that there were two dragon kings, since prior to this, Val's presence was kept mostly secret.

You ready? Sid asked.

Val nodded.

Prometheus. Come forward please.

The mass of dragons shifted, and Theo made his way to the front. He stopped a few feet from Sid. Val wondered if he knew what was about to happen. Sid spoke so everyone could hear. There would be no escaping for Theo. Even if Sid couldn't kill him, someone would.

We have irrefutable evidence that you are the human killer.

Theo backed up a few feet, and the rest of the dragons tightened the circle so he couldn't escape.

What evidence is that?

You are the only royal dragon that was in Hawaii when a human was eaten. Same thing with Alaska. There was a witness to the death in California. Plus, you were missing the weekend my father died. It was you. How could you kill my father?

Obsidian, I didn't do it.

Prove it.

I can't. Theo bared his teeth. *You made a mistake with Marc. How do you know you aren't making another mistake?*

I see no other possibility.

Without warning, Theo lunged at Sid. He snapped at Sid's neck, but Sid took flight before he could get at him. Theo leapt in the air and within seconds was all over Sid. Val and a few others took to the air as well. Theo slashed at Sid, and Sid snapped at Theo's flank, taking out a chunk of flesh. Theo roared, letting out a jet of hot gold flames. Then he turned around going after Sid's tail.

The flying dragons hovered around the fighting dragons. Val would intervene when he needed to, but for now, he watched, fascinated by how well Sid fought.

A gunshot ran out, and for a second everyone froze. A bright red stain blossomed on Sid's flank. Everything seemed to move in slow motion. Sid jerked around. Then he fell from the sky.

Val didn't even wait for Sid's body to hit the ground. He turned on Theo and went for the kill shot. Theo didn't see him coming. Val clamped his jaws around the top of Theo's head, and without hesitation, tore it from Theo's body. Blood exploded over him, but he didn't care. Didn't even want to relish in the victory. He dropped the head and raced for the ground, hoping against hope Sid would be okay.

CHAPTER 27

HAZEL AND ASPEN both had out binoculars and tried to watch the scene, but all they could see was the back side of several hundred dragons. The action was in the middle of the circle.

"Any idea what's going on?"

Aspen shrugged. "I just hope they kill Prometheus. I can't believe he did this."

"Did you know him?"

Aspen nodded. "He was Obsidian's best friend." Hazel thought for a second. Didn't Val say that he was Sid's best friend? Somehow those were connected.

Out of nowhere several dragons in the middle of the circle took flight. Hazel jerked her binoculars back up to her eyes and watched a black and gold dragon fight. Even from a distance they looked huge. Fangs and claws were slashing at one another. Hazel remembered her flight. Those claws had held her tight. She shuddered as she saw those same claws tear through dragon flesh.

"The black one is Obsidian right?"

"Yeah. The gold is Prometheus."

"Do you know the others?" Hazel asked, wondering how connected Aspen was to the dragons.

"A few. I don't recognize most of the gold ones."

A deafening shot rang out above them. Both Aspen and Hazel covered their ears, and then Hazel watched in horror as the black dragon fell to the earth. Paul promised he wouldn't miss, but he shot the wrong dragon.

Aspen ran.

Hazel was right on her heels. She couldn't let Aspen go out there on her own. The dragons parted for her as they ran through the crowd.

They reached Obsidian at the same time as the other black dragon touched down next to him. Aspen pressed her hands up against the gaping wound on his side, but blood gushed out around her fingers. Tears poured down her face.

"Sid, Sid, you can't die."

Hazel moved forward to help, placing her own hands around Aspen's, the warm blood coating her hands in seconds. Aspen continued to sob.

"Can you change?" Aspen asked the dragon. "It will be easier to stop the flow of blood."

The black dragon shuddered under their hands, and his body shrank. It wasn't Obsidian who lay there bleeding, but Sid.

Hazel backed away and brought her hand up to her mouth to suppress her scream. In her wildest imaginations she never thought this was possible. She spun around and saw dragons changing all over the field. Some wore modern day clothes, but others looked like they belonged in the Victorian era or early 1800s. Soon the only dragons left were a red one, Runa, and her mother. As one, they all dropped to the knees and bowed.

A woman in a pioneer dress approached. She tore strips of fabric from her massive skirt.

"Excuse me, Your Majesty, but I think I can help."

Aspen was still pressing her hands on the wound on Sid's chest. She looked up.

"Please. Anything you can do."

The woman ripped off a few more strips from her skirt and set to work. A handful of other women came forward and offered their services as well. Each addressed Aspen as "Your Majesty."

Aspen watched them work, holding Sid's hand. Hazel crouched down next to her.

"Why are they acting like you are some sort of royalty or something?"

Aspen gave her a weak smile. "Because I'm the queen of the dragons."

Hazel shook her head and clenched her fists. "No, that's not possible." What was Aspen telling her? That she was a dragon? She couldn't be. She was her sister.

Hazel stood, and Aspen looked up at her.

"Yes, it is. The dragon queen is always human. Sid's the king. He chose me."

Hazel backed away. She was in a nightmare or something. This couldn't be real.

A hand touched her shoulder. She spun and found Val. Bile threatened to rise.

"Are you like them?" she asked, pointing to the sea of humans.

He nodded. "I'm sorry I didn't tell you."

Hazel shook her head. She didn't know what to think, but she felt broken inside. Like someone had removed her heart.

Val knelt down next to Aspen. "You could heal him, you know."

Aspen stared at him with wide eyes for a second. "This is too big of a wound. I've never done more than a scratch before."

Val laid his hands over Aspen's, whose were clutching at Sid's.

"You have to try."

Aspen nodded. She let go of Sid's hands and pressed her hands on his wound. She squeezed her eyes shut for a second. Then she gasped, opened her eyes, and removed her hands. Gingerly, she lifted up the fabric covering the wound. The hole that had been there seconds ago was gone. Aspen let out a yelp of joy, then she collapsed on Sid's chest and sobbed.

Val stood up and approached Hazel. She backed away, not wanting him to touch her.

Val flinched but stopped. "I've got to take Sid to the woodland dragons to make sure he's completely healed. Aspen will come with. My father can take you back to the house. We'll talk when I get back."

Val pointed to the bright red dragon behind him, and Hazel felt the blood drain from her face. No way in hell was she getting on a dragon. Val changed into a massive black dragon, and Hazel's head spun. She took a few deep breaths so she didn't succumb to the desire to vomit. Scrawled across Val's ankle in bright green script was her name. What had he done to her? Why had he marked her?

She waited for Aspen to climb onto his back, and the other women helped lift Sid up with her. Then Val spread his wings and took off. Hazel disappeared among the crowd.

She hiked out to where they left the Hummers and sighed a breath of relief when she saw Paul leaning against the only remaining Hummer.

"Where did everyone go?" she asked.

"After I shot the wrong dragon, I ordered the troops to retreat. I watched long enough to see that they still killed the right dragon, then I bailed. Where's Aspen?"

"She'll be staying with the dragons. Thanks for waiting."

So he hadn't witnessed hundreds of dragons turning human. How convenient for the dragons. Hazel desperately wanted to talk to someone about it, but she wasn't sure how she could without sounding like a crazy person.

"On a scale of one to ten, how pissed are they that I shot the black one?"

"Not much was said. They were focusing on saving his life. But I'd say pretty pissed."

"Is he going to live?"

Hazel nodded.

Paul exhaled. "I'm still in trouble, but at least I didn't kill one I wasn't supposed to."

Hazel looked down at her hands. She'd wiped most of the blood off, but there was still some caked in her fingernails.

"Look, this has been a really long and strange day. Do you mind taking me home?"

"Sure, Hazel. Anything for you."

Hazel didn't want to talk on the way home, but Paul blathered on.

"After I drop you off, I need to go report to my supervisor. But, Hazel, that was surreal in there. I've never seen so many dragons. Have you?"

"No," she said and kept her gaze fixed on the trees flying by. Val was a dragon. She loved him, and he had lied to her. She thought she'd finally found someone worth settling down with, but he wasn't even human.

"So, are you going out to dinner with Val? Celebrate the loss of the human killer?"

Hazel shuddered as she remembered how the black dragon, who was Val, had ripped off the head of the gold dragon.

"Val and I aren't together anymore."

"Oh yeah? You want to go out to dinner with me then?"

Hazel's first reaction was hell no. But did she really want to stay home and replay the horror she witnessed in her mind over and over again? Paul could distract her. Save her from having to think about it for a few hours at least.

"Only under one condition."

"Anything for you."

"I don't want to hear the word dragon."

Paul dropped her off, and she made a beeline for the bathroom. She didn't want to talk to her parents. Not yet. She knew she'd have to face them before she went out again, but she desperately needed to be alone for a few minutes.

In the shower, Hazel scrubbed at the blood under her fingernails. She felt betrayed in every way possible. Val, who she'd finally given her heart to, broke it. He lied to her. Kept the most important thing from her. The fact that he wasn't even human. Hazel struggled to even comprehend that idea. Tears threatened to fall, but she kept them in. She didn't want to give Val the satisfaction that he'd hurt her. She knew he couldn't see her, but she still didn't want to give into the pain. The betrayal.

She was blow-drying her hair when her mom knocked on the bathroom door.

"Paul's here."

"Tell him I'll be down in a few minutes."

"Paul said they finally killed the dragon that's been plaguing us."

Hazel nodded. "Yeah, I was there. Saw it myself."

"Why were you there?"

"Because I wasn't going to let Aspen and Paul go without me."

"Where's Aspen?"

Hazel rolled her eyes. "With Sid. If I see her, I'll have her call you."

There was another person who broke her heart. How could Aspen keep all of this from her? She knew what Val was, and she didn't say a word. Not to mention this whole queen of the dragons thing.

Paul waited downstairs and helped her put her coat on.

"What do you want to do?" he asked when they got in the car.

"Anything to take my mind off what I saw today."

"Yeah, those dragons fighting was pretty scary. How about we grab some takeout and go back to my place and watch a movie. Something funny."

"That sounds amazing."

The movie was slapstick and funny and perfect for forgetting things she didn't want to think about. She curled into Paul's side, and he held her tight. She felt safe. Normal. This was a life she could handle. Nothing exciting, but secure. Now that she'd had a taste of commitment with Val, she realized she was done flitting around. She wanted to settle down. She wanted a real relationship. Paul would give her that. He wouldn't blink an eye. He probably still had the ring he proposed with before she fled to Hawaii.

The movie ended in the middle of her thoughts. Paul flicked off the television.

"Do you want me to find another movie?"

She shook her head, gave him a wicked grin, pulled his head down, and kissed him.

CHAPTER 28

VAL SAT AT the kitchen table with Aspen and Sid. The healing had been quick, and Sid was able to fly back on his own. Aspen stayed glued to his side. Val had never seen her so scared.

None of them said much. A few minutes later Pearl entered the room.

"The third black dragon has been spotted."

Sid jerked his head around. "Where?"

"Northern California. An eagle saw him, but when the dragons went in search of him, they couldn't find him."

Sid turned back to Val. "It's time to get this show on the road. Hazel needs to be made queen so we can focus on the third king. We don't know when the war will start. It could be years from now, or it could be tomorrow. We need to be prepared."

"I told Hazel to meet me here."

Aspen shook her head. "I just got a message from my mom. She went out with Paul tonight."

Val's heart clenched. "Why would she go out with him?"

Aspen frowned. "She didn't seem too happy to find out you were a dragon. She's probably just processing. I'm sure she feels like she can't talk to me or you. Let's give her the night, and we'll find her tomorrow. Convincing her to be queen though is not going to be easy."

Jealousy reared in his chest. "But she's out with another man. I should go get her."

"Don't do that. You'll just chase her away. Let her be tonight. We probably all ought to get some sleep. I thought things would get easier once the human killer was dead, but it looks like it will be just as crazy for the next several months or even years."

Sid nodded. "I could definitely use some sleep."

Val didn't want to go to sleep. He wanted to find Paul's house and convince Hazel to come home with him.

Sid put his hand on Val's shoulder. "I know what you're thinking, man. Just leave it. Give her a day to figure things out."

Reluctantly, Val went upstairs, showered, and went to bed. He didn't think he'd be able to sleep, but it came quickly. He hadn't realized how exhausted he was.

Light filled the room, and Val squinted his eyes against the brightness. It took a second for his eyes to adjust, but when it did, he saw Hazel standing in the doorway. Her hair stuck out in every direction, black streaks smeared her splotchy cheeks, and fresh tears fell. Her lips pressed in a straight line, and her eyes narrowed at him.

Without a word, she ripped off her sock and pointed to her ankle where his name was scrawled.

"What the hell did you do to me?"

He was so glad to see her he didn't think. He pulled her close and smashed his lips against hers. She'd come back to him. Sid had been right to let her have some time. She returned the kiss but then stiffened against his body and pulled away.

"No. You can't do this to me. I want to know what the hell this means and how I can get rid of it."

CHAPTER 29

"**Y**OU CAN'T."

Hazel spun, and saw Aspen standing in the doorway.

"Oh no, not you too."

"I told you. Not my secret to share."

Hazel rounded on her. "Not your secret? You're the queen of the effing dragons, and you didn't think I had a right to know that?"

Aspen shook her head. "No one knows. I knew I'd have to tell you eventually, but we had the human killer to take care of, Rowan missing, and the fact that you don't like dragons. You have to admit it was a lot."

Hazel stomped her foot like small child. "I don't care. I had a right to know. About all of this. I still don't understand."

"Well, now that you've woken the whole house, let's go talk in the theater room. It's more comfortable, and we'll be there for a while."

"What time is it?" Val asked from behind her.

"About two a.m." She couldn't look at him. She didn't understand the spell he'd cast over her. But kissing Paul felt wrong, and she knew she'd never love him the way she loved Val. She had left and drove around for hours trying to make sense of things. But sense could not be found.

"Fine. But no more lies." She stormed off for the theater room.

Val, Aspen, and Sid joined her a few minutes later.

"Can I sit next to you?" Val asked.

"No." Hazel crossed her arms and nodded her head in the direction of the opposite side of the couch. She was far too wound up to sit near anyone.

She sat alone on one side of the couch. The other three sat together. Aspen spoke first.

"Your mark will never go away because you are in love with Val. That will never change."

"Why did you do that me?" she asked Val.

Aspen spoke before he had a chance. "He didn't do it to you. You did to yourself. If Val had fallen in love with you first, you would've never seen the mark. But you fell in love with him."

Hazel ran a hand through her hair. "That's impossible. It was one kiss on an airplane."

Aspen grinned at her. "That must've been some kiss."

Hazel glowered at her. This wasn't any time to be making jokes.

"Are you saying I will never be able to love anyone else?" Hazel tried to wrap her head around that concept. The idea that she would never love another. In a way she'd already known this, but hearing the words out loud made it real.

"I'm saying you won't want to. Even now, you want to be with Val. Right?"

Hazel sighed. It was difficult to even look at him. "Is this some weird magic or something that dragons have?"

"Something like that. But I want you to know that it was you who chose to love him. He didn't do anything to you. I loved Sid first. When my mark showed up, it didn't have his name, and he didn't get one until after he fell in love with me. Rowan has one too, but it doesn't have a name because she doesn't love him back."

"Wait, are you saying that Skye chick is a dragon?"

Aspen nodded.

"Does Rowan know?"

"Yeah. He took it about as well as you did. But he got over it."

Hazel didn't believe her. But she figured if Rowan could get over it, she would eventually as well. But that wouldn't happen tonight.

Sid leaned forward on the couch. "Hazel, we need your help."

"Excuse me?"

"The dragons are about to go to war, and we need you to help us fight."

Hazel snorted. "I saw the fighting you did today, and I don't see how I can help."

"Dragon kings get an enormous amount of strength from their queens. Aspen became my queen because she loves me, but also because I needed her. I have more strength than any other living dragon because of what she gave me. You could do the same for Val."

Hazel creased her eyebrows. "What are you talking about?"

Val crossed over to her side of the couch and took her hands in his own. "I'm also a dragon king."

"How many kings are there?"

"Normally only one. But right now there are three. We haven't found the third one yet, but a couple of eagles spotted him in northern California. This is the fulfillment of a prophecy given thousands of years ago. Sid is right. I need your strength. But more than that, Hazel, I'm so in love with you. I don't want to spend another second without you. I would be honored if you would consent to become my queen. Not because I need you, but because I love you."

Hazel took a deep breath. She didn't know how to respond. She loved Val with every fiber of her being. She knew that. She was also furious with him. She opened her mouth to respond when Runa crashed on the floor in between them all.

"What is the meaning of this? Why are you having an important meeting without me?" Runa looked livid. Her face had gone a brilliant shade of red.

Aspen burst into laughter, and Sid followed suit. Val kept his eyes trained on Hazel though, his face expectant. Hazel couldn't find the words she needed to say, so instead, she leaned forward and kissed him.

CHAPTER 30

VAL COULDN'T believe his fortune. Hazel hadn't hesitated for even a second. He felt like he was in a dream.

"I'm going to summon an eagle. We'll have the council meet us tomorrow morning and take care of the gifting and bonding ceremony," Sid said.

Aspen jerked. "Will she have to go through the testing?"

Sid shook his head. "One of the things the council and I agreed upon was that the new queens would not have to submit to the testing since we already have one queen who did. But she will still need to be given the gifts so that Val can have them."

Hazel clenched at Val's hands. He wished he could tell what she was thinking.

Sid stood. "We should all go to bed. Tomorrow's going to be a long day. As soon as the ceremony is over, we need to go find the third king."

Val pulled Hazel up and led her back to his room. She crawled into bed and cuddled up to him, resting her face on his chest. He stroked her hair.

"You don't seem too freaked out by all this," he said.

She chuckled. "Oh, I'm definitely freaked out. I know I was super angry when I arrived tonight, but I had already made the decision I wanted to be with you.

"Why? I'm glad you did, but it doesn't make sense."

She slid her hand up his shirt, and he tensed, but she was still relaxed. "You know I went out with Paul tonight, right?"

"Yeah, Aspen told me."

She was lightly running her fingers along his stomach, and it was incredibly distracting.

"Well, I kissed him."

He unconsciously clenched his fists.

"Ouch," Hazel said.

"Oh, sorry." He'd grabbed her hair by mistake. He relaxed his fists again. "Why'd you kiss him?"

"Because I was angry and hurt, and I wanted to forget about you."

"What happened?" He didn't want to know the answer to this, but he had to hear it.

"It was awful."

Val snorted. "Really?"

Hazel shimmied off his chest and propped herself up on her elbows so she was facing him. "Yes, really. No one will ever taste as sweet as you do. Not to mention that even though I didn't want to admit it, I'm totally in love with you. Much more so than I ever was with Teddy. Speaking of, it's going to be awkward seeing him around here." Hazel froze. "Wait, is he a dragon too?"

Val wondered how she'd take this news. "He was."

"What's that supposed to mean?"

"Uh, I killed him this afternoon."

"That was you? And him?"

"Yeah."

"Huh. At some point I'm going to have to reconcile the fact that I was once in love with a serial killer."

"Hopefully not tonight." He didn't want to spend the rest of the night rehashing her relationship with Theo.

She wiggled forward and kissed him lightly. "No, definitely not tonight. Now, can you explain to me what's going to happen tomorrow? Because I am a little weirded out by the fact that I'm about to become a queen."

"I don't really want to talk much tonight. But I promise I will tell you anything you want to know in the morning." Val flipped her over so he was hovering over her. Her eyes had a bright sparkle, and she pulled his head down toward her. She kissed him deeply, and he knew he'd be happy to never leave that room.

CHAPTER 31

AFTER BREAKFAST the next day, an eagle tapped on the window. Sid opened it, stared at the eagle, and closed the window.

"They council will meet us in the king's cave in about thirty minutes. You ready?"

Hazel nodded her head even though she really wanted to shake it. She was ready to be with Val forever, but she still wasn't sure about the dragon thing. Val had explained what he knew about the ceremony, which wasn't much. Aspen probably would've been a better resource, but Hazel hadn't wanted to leave Val's side, and she felt weird asking Aspen personal questions in front of him.

The four of them went out the back door with Runa following.

"Another queen, yay!" Runa bobbed up and down excitedly. "Do you like dragons now?" she asked Hazel.

"No. Not really."

Runa dropped to the ground. She stretched her neck high, but she still didn't reach above Hazel's knee.

"But you're about to become a queen."

"I know. But that's because I love Val, not because I care for the dragons."

"But Val's a dragon."

"Well, he's not perfect now, is he?" Hazel didn't know how to explain to Runa that she was only doing this for Val.

Aspen chuckled next to her. "They'll grow on you. Runa, don't worry, my sister will be a good queen."

"Not like you, she won't."

"I'm only interested in making Val happy. From what I've heard, that's all that really matters."

Aspen nudged her. "It's much more than that. But over time, you'll learn, and I'm sure you'll come to like them. I'm glad you don't have to go through the testing though. That was awful."

"What'd you have to do?"

"I was tortured, blinded, had my mind probed, and was seduced. It was the worst several hours of my life. But I survived, and that meant Sid did as well. It was worth it. Come on, it's time to go."

Hazel gripped Aspen's hand. She and Aspen would need to spend some time together when this was all over and talk. The things her sister had gone through in the last few months were unthinkable.

Hazel watched as Val's body changed from human to dragon. He brought his head down and blinked his deep brown eyes at her. They were so dark they nearly blended in with his black scales.

You ready?

"Was that you?"

Val's body shook. *Yes, you can talk to me with your mind as well if you try hard enough. We'll practice on the way to the cave. Now climb on up.*

"You want help?" Aspen asked.

Hazel shook her head. She wanted to do this on her own.

Her hands trembled as she placed them on the smooth scales. She threw her leg over his neck and hoisted herself up. It was easier than she thought it would be. She gripped his neck tight when he spread his wings and took off. Suddenly her fear of flying overcame her. Her heart began to race, and all of her muscles tensed. She squeezed her eyes shut and tried to take deep breaths.

You okay?

She shook her head against his body, but she knew he couldn't see her.

I wish I could kiss you right now.

She almost laughed. That would make it all better. The flight seemed to take forever. But soon the light changed. Hazel peeked and saw they were in a cave. One with ruby studded walls.

Val touched down in the middle of a cavern.

"We beat the council," Aspen said, scrambling off Sid's back. She stood below Hazel. "Getting off is harder than getting on. You have to slide down."

Hazel stumbled a little when she hit the ground. Val changed into a human and immediately brought her in for a kiss.

"What was that for?" Hazel asked.

"Because I couldn't comfort you on the flight."

Aspen giggled. "Oh yeah, I forgot Hazel doesn't like to fly. Oh, here they come."

A sparkly silver dragon flew above them, followed by a bright red one.

"That's Pearl. She's Sid's sister. Behind her is Eros. Are you related to him, Val?"

"Not that I know of."

"Val's a fire dragon," Aspen continued. Three more dragons flew in after them. "The yellow one is Xanthous. I like him. The blue is Kairi. Be glad you don't have to go through her test." Aspen shivered. "Sequoia is the purple and green. Oh, and look, there comes Anasazi. He's a canyon. That speck behind him is Nedra. He's blind." Aspen creased her eyebrows. "Hey, Sid. Did they replace Winerva?"

No. We'll have to do without an arctic dragon.

"What happened to Winerva?" Hazel asked.

"I killed her. It was an accident, but still, the arctic dragons aren't happy with us."

"How do you accidentally kill a dragon? Especially an arctic dragon. They're enormous," Val asked.

"She tried to kill me, and I had a sword in my hand."

"Aspen, you and I are going to have a long talk when we get home tonight," said Hazel.

"Tomorrow. Tonight you and loverboy will sleep in the king's chambers. Come on. They want to get started."

The three of them approached the dragons, who had formed a half circle. Runa flew right behind them. Sid was already standing in front of the council.

Xanthous approached her.

"There has been a change of plans."

"What do you mean?" Aspen asked, clutching at Hazel's arm.

"Obsidian convinced us to do away with the testing, but truthfully we weren't entirely comfortable with that. We need to make sure she will be able to withstand being a dragon queen."

Sid stepped forward. "Excuse me? We agreed that a testing would not be necessary. Aspen was lucky she survived. We don't have time to train the new queens. Their sole purpose is so the new kings get the gifts they need."

Xanthous shook his bright yellow head. "You think that is their only purpose? You have a lot to learn, young king. No, they are much more than simply carriers for the gifts. We need to make sure she's fitting. We've developed a test that will allow us to judge the more important aspects. She will be in no physical danger."

"Explain."

"Ah, that would ruin the test now, wouldn't it? Suffice it to say, we will test her on compassion, temptation, secrecy, and persuasion. Pearl will monitor her emotions, and Anasazi will watch her thoughts and convey them to the rest of us."

Sid deferred to Val. "What do you think?"

"I think it's up to Hazel."

Hazel jerked her head up. She wasn't sure what she thought. She didn't know what this test would entail, but listening to Aspen talk about her own wasn't encouraging. Then again, she needed to prove herself.

"If that is what it takes to become queen, then yes."

"Fantastic," said Xanthous. "I do hope you'll be as entertaining as your sister was. Obsidian, will you take Aspen and Valentine up to the observation area?"

Val gave Hazel a lingering kiss. "You don't have to do this."

"Of course I do. They said I wouldn't be in any danger. I can handle it."

CHAPTER 32

TWO DRAGONS holding a cage flew into the pit. They set it down on the ground in front of Hazel, and she paled when she saw that it contained a human. Not just any human either. Paul.

She ran to the bars. "Are you okay? Why are you in there?"

Xanthous stepped around the side of the cage. "Because he tried to kill our king."

"He was trying to kill the human killer."

"But he didn't. He shot Obsidian."

"This is ridiculous. Let him go." Outrage filled Hazel's mind.

"Are you sure that's what you want? What if his sentence is all that stands between you and Valentine? If we let him go, we may not let you become queen. Think carefully of what you want."

Hazel didn't know what to think. On one hand, Paul didn't mean to shoot Obsidian, but on the other hand, she could see how they might think otherwise.

She took a deep breath and stepped away from Paul's cage.

"Exactly what is it you want from me?"

"We want you to make a decision. You'll be queen. This is part of your duties. What should happen to this man who thinks it is okay to shoot at innocent dragons? Keep in mind that your thoughts and feelings will be monitored."

Oh great, so even her thoughts could condemn her.

She decided to start easy. "Look, Sid is fine. There is no reason for Paul to be held here. Let him go."

"You would let him go? What if Obsidian had died? Would your answer be any different?"

Hazel stopped short. Would it? It should be. Obsidian was her sister's love. That deserved something.

"Of course that would change my response. If Obsidian died, everything would be different."

"But Paul's actions would be no different. The crime is still the same."

Hazel looked over at the cage. Paul was looking around like he couldn't see or hear anything that was going on.

"What's wrong with him? Why won't he look at me?"

"Because he is in an enchantment. In thirty seconds, we'll remove that enchantment. You will be able to see and converse with him. You cannot tell him of Val or your role among our kingdom. Our secrets must be kept. Once the enchantment is lifted, you'll have fifteen minutes."

"Fifteen minutes to do what?"

"To decide his fate."

Hazel barely had time to process those words when she saw the light shift, and Paul saw her.

"Hazel, what are you doing here?"

She went to the cage. "Are you okay?" she asked.

He nodded. "What am I doing in here?"

"I don't....don't know." She didn't know how to tell him about the dragons without revealing the secrets they didn't want revealed. "How did you get in there?"

"I'm not sure. I went to bed, and then I woke up in here a couple of hours ago. Can you get me out?"

"I don't think so." She sat down in front of the cage and studied him. He didn't deserve to be in there. What he did was an accident. But Xanthous's words floated around in her head. His actions were the same, no matter the outcome.

"Can I ask you a question?" Hazel asked.

Paul sat. "Sure."

"If you were up in the tree again with that gun, but you knew that you'd hit the wrong dragon, would you still pull the trigger."

"Come on, Hazel, they are just dragons."

"You didn't answer my question."

"Yeah, I would. If there was any chance at all that I would get the human killer. I had to."

"Why?"

"Because those were my orders."

"What? To kill the human killer?"

Paul snorted. "No, to see if the gun would work."

Hazel stood and backed away from the cage. That was not the response that she expected.

"And what do you think? Did it work?"

"It needs a few modifications, but overall the effect was desired. Next time it should do what it was intended to do."

"What is that?"

"Kill the dragons. Come on, Hazel. They can't be allowed to live." Hazel wanted to tell him to shut up, to stop talking because he was only guaranteeing that no matter what she said, he'd be killed.

"They took care of the dragon that was killing humans."

"Sure, this time. They are too big, too threatening to be here. They should've died out with the dinosaurs. There's no place for them in the human world."

A week ago, she would've agreed with him, but now she knew better. Plus she didn't want Val to die.

"So what's going to happen to them?"

"Once the guns are done being modified, we're going hunting."

Hazel recoiled, but she also knew there was no way they could kill him now. Believe it or not, he'd just ensured his survival. She figured she had about five minutes left. Five minutes to convince him that he was wrong.

"Paul, you can't mean that. They are basically peaceful."

He laughed. "Since when do you say stuff like that? I'd swear I'm talking to Aspen and not you."

"Maybe she got to me."

"Maybe she did."

The next few minutes passed faster than she had hoped, but she hadn't made any headway with Paul. Hazel could tell the second time was up.

"Hazel, where'd you go?" Paul was looking wildly around, and Xanthous appeared in front of her again.

"So, have you made a decision for that despicable man?"

"I have." Xanthous would not like what she would say. "Let him go."

With the exception of the orange dragon, the dragons around her shifted and colored smoke poofed out of several snouts.

Calm down. Hear her out.

The dragons all stilled, and Hazel knew the canyon dragon had spoken to them all.

Pearl, does she mean to deceive?

Not that I can tell.

Very well, Hazel, tell them why you want to let him go.

"Because he's obviously a pawn in this plan. If you kill him, you'll never find the guns that he is speaking of until it's too late. By letting him go, you can follow him and destroy the guns before they have a chance to use them against you. It makes no sense to kill him or keep him locked up."

Xanthous cocked his head. "So you would have us let him go to protect us?"

"Yes, I would."

"Pearl, does she speak the truth?"

I believe she does.

"Very well. Let us talk for a moment. Obsidian, you can come back down."

They lifted Paul's cage out of the pit, and Sid, Val, and Aspen joined them from the top of the cavern. Aspen threw her arms around Hazel. "That was amazing. Though I have to say, you got off easy."

"That didn't seem so easy."

Val changed to a human form and slid his arm around her waist as Xanthous approached her.

"You passed the test. You showed immense compassion for both the dragons and the humans. Paul was the one person who could possibly change your mind because you care for him a great deal, yet neither Pearl nor Anasazi sensed your desire to be with him. In this, you resisted temptation. You also did not reveal our secrets to him. Then you persuaded us to keep that despicable man alive. You do not love the dragons, and yet you seem to only desire what is best for us. I still sense some hesitancy from you. Are you willing to accept this life among the dragons?"

"I am."

He studied her for a moment and then seemed to accept her sincerity. "Let us begin. I will start by giving you my gift. From me, you'll receive the ability to converse in all tongues and with any species."

He touched his snout to her hand, and she felt a warmth flow through her. She tried not to think of the ramifications of his gift.

The purple dragon with the bright green wings approached her next. *I give you the gift to heal those around you.* She brushed her forehead, and another thread of warmth flowed through Hazel. Now she understood how Aspen had healed Sid on the field.

The brown dragon came next. *From me, you are given strength.*

Followed by the orange dragon. *I give you the ability to hear the thoughts of those around you.*

Then the blue dragon. *I give you the power to shield your mind from unwanted watchers.*

The red dragon didn't even bother to speak to her. He just touched her head with his snout. She'd have to ask Val later what his gift did.

The silver dragon came last. *I give you the gift to feel the emotions of those around you.*

Hazel was now buzzing with the thoughts and feelings of everyone around her. She couldn't make heads or tails of it.

"You okay?" Val asked.

Hazel nodded. "Is there any way to block out the thoughts?"

The orange dragon came forward once again. *You must build a shield in your mind. Think of a brick wall. It is not difficult.*

Hazel consciously built a wall around her mind, and immediately the voices disappeared.

"Whew. That's better. Now what?"

"Now we become bonded. You ready?"

She smiled at him, and Sid approached them. *This works best if you embrace one another.*

"No complaints here." Val brought her into his arms. She clutched at his back and rested her face on his chest.

She watched as Sid opened his mouth and bright white flames spewed forth. For a half second terror filled her, but as the flames engulfed her, she realized that it wasn't hot. She felt herself merging with Val. It was a strange sensation. His memories became hers, and almost immediately she wanted to ask him about them. Within seconds it was over.

She untangled herself from Val, and Aspen caught her up in a hug. "Now, we have two queens in the family. I think it's time to tell Mom."

"She won't believe us."

We have company.

The voice had come from the canyon dragon. Everyone turned to face the entrance to the cavern. In flew another black dragon. Val pulled her back and whispered fiercely in her ear. "Go hide. We don't know if this dragon is safe or not. He's been deliberately hiding from us, and we don't know why. Take Aspen and go."

Hazel took his hand in her own. "I'm your queen now. I'll stand next to you, thank you very much."

The dragon hovered for a second before dropping to the floor. It took a moment for Hazel's eyes to take it in, but soon she realized that he had a person on his back.

The young man slid off of the dragon. In spite of the cold, he wore only a t-shirt, with ripped jeans and Converse sneakers. His blonde hair was spiked, and his brilliant green eyes sparkled in the dim light. Hazel couldn't help but admire the muscles that rippled as he reached up and patted the dragon on its neck. The young man stepped toward them, and Aspen squealed.

"Rowan!"

Aspen raced for him and embraced him. Hazel right behind her. He didn't look like himself, but Hazel didn't care. Rowan was alive. He crushed her in a hug.

"You scared the hell out of me," she mumbled into his shoulder. She let go of him. "Where have you been?"

He grinned. "That's a long story."

"Yeah, and I expect it has to do with that black dragon over there. How'd you find him when the rest of the dragons couldn't?" Aspen asked.

Rowan snorted. "Him?" Then he turned around. "Love, I think it's time you revealed yourself."

The black dragon rapidly shrunk into the most beautiful woman Hazel had ever seen.

"Skye?" Aspen looked at the girl with confusion.

"The one and only." She waltzed over and put arm around Rowan's waist. "Have we got a story to tell you."

ABOUT THE AUTHOR

KIMBERLY LOTH CAN'T decide where she wants to settle down. She's lived in Michigan, Illinois, Missouri, Utah, California, Oregon, and South Carolina. She finally decided to make the leap and leave the U.S. behind for a few years. She spent two wild years in Cairo, Egypt. Currently, she lives in Shenzhen, China with her husband and two kids. She is a middle school math teacher by day (please don't hold that against her) and YA author by night. She loves romantic movies, chocolate, roses, and crazy adventures. *Valentine* is her eighth novel..

ACKNOWLEDGEMENTS

A S ALWAYS, there are so many people to thank for their help on this and other books. If I have left you off and you helped me, I'm so, so sorry. I know I'm forgetting some pretty important people. One of these days I'll learn to keep a list while I'm working.

Will, thank you for allowing me to follow my dreams. I never imagined we'd get this far.

Xandi and AJ, You two are the best kids a mother could ask for. Thank you for supporting me and being good kids so I don't have to worry :).

I can't forget to thank my family (all of you) but especially Mom, Matt, and Tiffany. Love you guys so much. I miss you more than words can express. We live way too far away from each other.

Virginia, you have become my whole world where books are concerned. I don't know how I would do this without you. Thanks for helping me out in every possible way. Love you!

Mandy, Kristin, and Karen, thank you for being my tribe. I couldn't do this with you.

Kelley, Suzi, Colleen, and Rebecca, you all are an amazing team. From editing to book and cover design, you ladies do a fantastic job.

To my proofreaders-Brittany, Tiffany and Donna. Thank you so much!!!

Finally a huge shoutout to all my fans and superfans. I want to give a special thank you to the following fans who go above and beyond in helping me promote my books—Amber Christiansen, Andrea Hubler, Angie Blankenship, Anne Loshuk, Beverly Laude, Brianna Snowball, Cameron Scott Wright, Cassandra Dahlin, Chris Radentz, Dawn F, Dawn Foster, Debbie Rodriguez, Jennifer McIntosh, Kristina Oden, Laurie Murray, Leona Bowman, Linda Lutchka, Michelle Collins, Michelle McLain, Mellissa Monteforte, Nancy McDonald, Nicole Kellum, Nikki, Patricia Bercaw, Roylyne Markos, Ruqayyah Hashmi, Samantha Murphy, Sarah Moon, Vivian Furch, Zoe Cannon, and Fi Pad.

Made in the USA
Middletown, DE
05 July 2018